ESCAPE FROM FORT ISAAC

When Lieutenant Elliott Stanton is unjustly convicted of rape, he is sentenced to a twelve-year stretch in Fort Isaac prison. His military career is in ruins and he is blamed for the tragic death of the woman he had planned to marry. But he somehow manages to escape and is hunted by men he previously fought alongside and who now despise and disown him. Stanton encounters further tragedy and hardship but vows to track down those who have blackened his name and robbed him of so much . . .

BILL WILLIAMS

ESCAPE FROM FORT ISAAC

Complete and Unabridged

LINFORD
Leicester

First published in Great Britain in 2003 by
Robert Hale Limited
London

First Linford Edition
published 2004
by arrangement with
Robert Hale Limited
London

The moral right of the author
has been asserted

British Library CIP Data

Williams, Bill, *1940* –
    Escape from Fort Isaac.—Large print ed.—
Linford western library
    1. Western stories
    2. Large type books
    I. Title
    823.9'2 [F]

    ISBN 1–84395–383–8

Published by
F. A. Thorpe (Publishing)
Anstey, Leicestershire

Set by Words & Graphics Ltd.
Anstey, Leicestershire
Printed and bound in Great Britain by
T. J. International Ltd., Padstow, Cornwall

This book is printed on acid-free paper

1

He stood tall with his head held high, just as he had done on the day he was commissioned nearly three years ago. His folks had been so proud as his name was called out on the parade ground at the West Point Military Academy: Lieutenant Elliott James Stanton. He was glad that his parents had stayed away from the court and that he had faced this alone. Today was all about shame and dishonour when he was found guilty of rape. The effects of weeks cooped up in a garrison cell being fed meagre rations of food had taken their toll. His rugged features were drawn, emphasizing the square jaw and broad nose. His dark brown eyes were dull and sad where they had once been lively, and his thick black curly hair, greasy and unkempt where it had once been immaculately groomed.

Many of the faces at the court martial were familiar to him and some had been friends, but now they had disowned him. Elliott could understand why Colonel Danvers would feel as he did, but not the others. Surely they must have known that he wouldn't have done such things. There had been no witnesses, except Eleanor Danvers, and she was dead. She had run towards a passing wagon for help after being raped, but had been dragged along under its wheels after she had fallen.

During the time that Elliott had been locked up in Fort Isaac, he'd reflected how within a year he would have married Eleanor and with her father's blessing. All his plans had been decimated just over a month ago when he was picnicking with Eleanor. They had talked of their future, about marriage, children, his career in the army and so many other things that day. She had looked more beautiful than ever, clearly excited by the talk of their future together. Her cheeks had been flushed and her large, blue eyes full of excitement and hope. But the last memory he had of her was a look of surprise as she had glanced over his shoulder, just before he received the blow to the side of his face.

★ ★ ★

'I'm sorry, Elliott, but I did my best,' said Lieutenant Jeremy Everson as he sat down after delivering his summing-up of the defence case.

Elliott was disappointed that Everson had put up such a poor performance on his behalf. There were things they had discussed that he had not raised; perhaps he had just forgotten them or maybe he thought they were not important. A more experienced legal man would have done better, but it wouldn't have changed the outcome.

Captain Owen J. Slattery, who had been assigned by the Judge Advocate to present the prosecution case, didn't hide his own personal feelings during his summing-up. The defendant had brutally savaged the lady whom he was supposed to have loved. Fearing the consequences of his behaviour he had tried to murder her, but she had managed to catch him off guard and somehow knock him unconscious. She must have been involved in an almighty struggle with her attacker, but she had clung to the button that she had ripped from his uniform. That button had come from the uniform of Elliott Stanton. She may have been killed by the hoofs of the horses and the wheels of the wagon, but another animal had been the real cause of her death that day.

When the Judge Advocate, General Daniel Compton, delivered his summing-up, he expressed regret that the law did not permit him to deliver a death sentence. It was the General's final words that hurt as much as the twelve-year prison sentence. They were the words that declared Lieutenant Elliott Stanton as a disgrace to the uniform of the US Cavalry.

'Let him rot in hell,' someone shouted from the court.

Elliott noted that Colonel Danvers, Eleanor's father and commanding officer of Fort Isaac showed no emotion, even though he must have hated him more than any other man in the courtroom.

Elliott was escorted from the court amidst a barrage of abuse. He would have to wait until he was back in his cell and the handcuffs had been removed before he could wipe away the spit from his face. He had never seen a woman spit before today, nor seen such venom in the eyes of people whom he was certain wished him dead. He wanted to scream his innocence, but knew that his cries would fall on deaf ears. How he wished that just one of his former friends would have believed him, offered him some hope that his nightmare would end. Everson had tried to give him some moral support, but probably only because it was part of his job. He had to defend him, but it didn't mean that he believed him. Why should he?

Elliott had slept very little during the night as the enormity of the sentence and the bleakness of what the future held for him tortured his mind. His main distress was not for himself but for his parents. The sentence would not come as a surprise to them but he was no longer the accused: he was now the guilty. Any last glimmer of hope that they might have cherished was now gone. He wondered if he would ever see them again. He knew that his folks were in good health, but anything might happen to them during the twelve years that he would be in prison. They had both endured a hard life as they battled with the rigours of settling in the west, but one thing was certain: their lives would never be the same again.

He didn't have much of an appetite, but he would need all his strength to cope with prison and he would force himself to eat food when it arrived. He would be picked on in prison, he knew that for sure. He had been an officer and some men would see it as a chance to get even for the times that they had suffered under the command of a bad officer. But worse than that, he would have the label of a rapist. Some men didn't need much of an excuse to torment others, but even good men who had wives, sweethearts, mothers or sisters would want to see him pay for what he was supposed to have done.

He had just finished looking at the faded photograph of his parents when he heard voices in the corridor.

'Hey, rapist, you got a visitor,' growled the guard.

Elliott was disappointed when he saw that it was Everson. He didn't dislike the man, but he didn't see any point in discussing the case again. It was over as far as he was concerned.

When Everson entered the cell, Elliott noted that his holster was empty and so there was no chance of him being tempted to snatch it, at least not

7

this time. He had thought long and hard about whether he should attempt to escape if he got the opportunity, and had decided that if a chance arose then he would take it. He wasn't going to be able to find the real rapist while he was locked up in prison.

'I'll spend the next few days going over things again, Elliott, but to be honest with you, we don't really have any grounds for appeal.'

'My only chance is to find the man who attacked Eleanor,' Elliott responded, 'and I'm never going to be able to that now.'

'I've tried asking around, but everyone's so convinced it was you they won't entertain the idea that it could have been anyone else.'

'That's what is so damned difficult to accept. I've lived and fought with those men. They know me and yet they all believe that I could do something so horrible. Why would I do such a thing? I would have been married to Eleanor before too long. Don't they question why I would want to do such a thing?'

'We've been through all this, Elliott, and you have got to accept that without a witness or the real culprit being exposed, nothing is going to change.'

'If I hadn't have been arrested that day, I would have hunted the man down until I found him, but I'll get him one day, even if I have to wait twelve years.'

Everson was beginning to feel uncomfortable and would be glad to get out of the cell. 'I'll come and see you again tomorrow, but you should prepare yourself for what lies ahead. If only Eleanor hadn't been clutching that button off your tunic, it might have been different.'

Lieutenant Everson rattled the bars of the cell to attract the attention of the prison guard.

'Will you be coming back, sir?' boomed Sergeant Nolan.

'Not today, Sergeant, but I'll be back tomorrow.'

'Right you are, sir. The prisoner will

still be here,' replied Nolan with a broad smile, and added, 'I will personally guarantee that.'

The two men exchanged salutes and Everson hurried away as Nolan approached Elliott's cell. Nolan was a brute of a man, barrel-chested and with a face that bore the marks of many bar-room brawls, but he was a fine soldier and despite his bullying was extremely popular with most of the men. He was a strict disciplinarian but could always be relied upon to support his men, especially if they got involved with a dispute with some greenhorn officer who tried to throw his weight about.

'Lieutenant Everson didn't help you much in court, did he?' Nolan gloated. 'Then again, perhaps his heart wasn't really in it. They tell me he used to be really sweet on Miss Eleanor himself when they were both back East.'

'He did his best,' replied Elliott, not giving Nolan the satisfaction of upsetting him. Eleanor had never mentioned that she knew Everson before and obviously Nolan was doing his best to annoy him. Sergeant Nolan enjoyed riling people, particularly officers. Most of them were useless and had things too easy. The army was just a game to them but to Nolan it was a serious business.

'I suppose it's about time for your meal,' Nolan sighed and glanced at the cell clock. 'What would you like? How about a nice piece of beef or perhaps some fresh fish? I'll send one of my men over to Colonel Danvers and see if he'll supply you with a bottle of vintage wine. I expect you developed some expensive tastes, you being an officer and mixing in high circles. But I forgot you're just a farmer's boy.'

'I'll have the wine later, Sergeant, but thanks for offering,' replied Elliott, determined not to let Nolan think that he was annoying him.

'Perhaps you'd prefer something more basic like another plate of beans, because that's all you'll be getting while you're in here.'

'You always did have a childish sense of humour, Sergeant. It's probably why you were never considered for a commission. Then again, you're not exactly an intelligent man, are you?'

Nolan glared at Elliott. He wanted to give him a good beating, a sort of farewell present — and he would before Stanton departed from Fort Isaac, but in the meantime he would annoy him as much as possible, so he said, 'By the way, I thought you ought to know that Cookie Smithson hates you just as much as I do. Miss Danvers was liked by everyone at the fort but Cookie had a real soft spot for her.'

'You don't need to remind me how well liked she was, Sergeant.'

'I'm just making conversation and I'd make the most of it if I were you. I daresay you're going to be spending a lot of time in solitary for your own protection because most men can't abide rapists. They hate them just as much as they do them Injuns. They get to thinking what men like you are up to with their women while they're cooped up inside. It makes them so mean and they'll think that by beating you up they are protecting their women. I believe that the guards turn the other way when they know a rapist is involved.'

'I'll face that if it happens, but they'll be picking on an innocent man.'

Stanton kept eye contact with his tormentor, and it was the bully who looked away and then sniggered. 'Yeah, yeah of course you're innocent. I keep forgetting. By the way, in all my years in the army I ain't ever met a man who picks his nose or spits as much as Cookie does. Anyway, that's enough chin-wagging for now, I'll go and organize that meal for you. Make sure you enjoy it, I don't think you'll need any salt.'

Elliott could still hear the Sergeant's laughter as he left the prison building.

The day after the verdict had been delivered, Captain Pearmain came to see Elliott and explained the details of his transfer to the state prison at

Pinnington Creek. He had never really liked Pearmain despite getting on well with him professionally. During social occasions he was inclined to belittle his wife Eloise and criticise her appearance, and would frequently brag about his past experiences with women. Pearmain was related to Eleanor on her father's side but there was no family resemblance. Pearmain was dark where she had been fair. He was the tallest man at the fort and had his uniforms specially tailored, and would visit the barber's every day to have the moustache that he was so proud of attended to. Pearmain was a handsome man and he and his short frumpy wife Eloise were an unlikely match — and the subject of a number of cruel jokes that circulated the fort. Elliott had been surprised that the captain had been so civil towards him considering his relationship to the Danvers family.

He would have liked to have believed Pearmain's assurances that he would be well treated on the trip to Pinnington

Creek, but he had his doubts. If he had been a betting man then he would have said that the odds were against him arriving there unharmed. The first fifty miles to the train depot would pass through a small section still known for isolated problems with the Indians, but he suspected that his main danger would come from those in the escort party. There might be some who would use the opportunity to desert, and would be prepared to kill him and Captain Pearmain if necessary.

As Pearmain was about to leave the cells, Elliott asked him if Eleanor had known Everson back East.

Pearmain reacted as though he was surprised by the question. 'Of course she did. In fact most of the family thought that they would marry one day but she went cool on him. I thought you must have known. Eleanor wasn't one for keeping secrets.'

Elliott frowned. 'No, I didn't know. I suppose she thought it was just a boy and girl relationship.'

'It was a bit more than that, old man. They were practically engaged. I'm surprised that Everson didn't tell you himself. It wasn't very ethical of him seeing as how he was your defence counsel. I did question his appointment with my uncle, but you can appreciate that he wasn't too interested in your welfare at the time and said that it didn't really matter because you were as guilty as sin.'

After Pearmain had left, Elliott brooded on the relationship between Eleanor and Everson. Elliott wondered if she had really loved him. Perhaps she never intended to actually marry him and would have ditched him before long as well. He tried to think back to when he had seen Everson and Eleanor together. Then he remembered that on the night of his engagement party he had found them alone on the Colonel's porch. Perhaps it was then that they had agreed to keep their past relation-ship quiet — but why? He cursed himself for having such doubts and for souring his memory of her.

Elliott had turned his thoughts to his parents and was wondering how they would cope, when he heard the jangle of the keys.

'Up you get, Stanton, you're leaving,' Nolan growled.

'But I'm not due to leave until tomorrow. Why didn't Captain Pearmain mention it when he was here?'

'When I say you are leaving, what I really meant to say is that you are a free man, by orders of Colonel Danvers.'

'Is this your idea of some kind of sick joke, Nolan? I don't know what tricks you are up to but I want to see an officer. I want to see Captain Pearmain.'

'Now listen, you rapist. As of now you're a civilian and I want you out of here. You get on that horse that's waiting outside and ride for your life. If you don't then I'll kill you now and say that you tried to escape.'

Nolan unlocked the cell door and pushed it open. 'Now get moving,' he ordered.

Elliott couldn't understand what was happening, except that he knew that he didn't have any choice but to go along with it. He didn't doubt that Nolan was serious about killing him. If Danvers wanted him dead then why didn't he let Nolan just do what he'd threatened and fake his escape?

Nolan grinned as Elliott passed him. He waited until the prisoner had almost reached the front door of the cell block before he called after him.

'You'll have a thirty-minute start then we'll be coming after you. If you get lucky you'll have your chance of freedom, at least for a while. You are now an escaped prisoner and you'll soon be a dead one.'

Elliott turned to see if the sergeant had followed him out, but there was no sign of him as he quickly mounted the horse and urged it towards the open gate. His heart pounded as he waited to be gunned down, knowing that it would bring further shame on his family. They might even think that his 'escape' attempt was a sign of his guilt.

He was surprised that Colonel Danvers had sanctioned his 'release' in this way, but it had no doubt been triggered by his bitterness towards the man he blamed for the death of his daughter. It had given Elliott some hope when he had none only a few minutes earlier and he would take his chance, even though he doubted if he would remain free or alive for very long.

The fort was deserted, or so it seemed. Perhaps his would-be killers were hiding, waiting for him to get closer to them before they opened fire. If he could just make it to the gate and beyond the firing range of the duty guard then he had a chance. There was no telling how many people would be aware of his arranged escape, perhaps no more than three or four, and that was why he was being allowed to get outside the fort to make his escape seem more genuine.

2

Nell Stanton hadn't needed to ask her husband Will what the verdict had been when he'd returned from the telegraph office earlier that day. Their life had been shattered by the news that their son had been accused of such a horrible crime. She knew that there wasn't the slightest chance that he could have done such a thing, but she had wondered if Will didn't harbour just a little doubt. Her husband had seen what the army could do to men. He had told her how quiet, even timid, men had changed into killers, their minds warped by the horrors that they witnessed and participated in.

Elliott had been mischievous, just like most boys, but he had grown into a God-fearing and good man. There were very few mothers alive who wouldn't defend their son against most accusations, no matter how much evidence was against them. Nell Stanton wasn't one of those mothers, and would have disowned him if he had been guilty as charged.

Elliott had been the first man from Traycora to become an officer. He wasn't just a source of pride to the Stantons but the whole town. As a boy he had been inseparable from his wooden gun and whenever he was in town with his pa, he would smile back at the men who would shout, 'Hi there, Soldier Boy'. Ma had given up trying to get folks to call him Elliott. By the time he was fifteen years old his pa had also given up any thought of Elliott being anything else but a soldier. The military had sad memories for Will, having lost two brothers during the Civil War. He had seen his older brother Ned die at Antietam Creek while they were fighting on the Union side, and found out later that his brother Danny had drowned while crossing the Potamac River with the

Confederate army that was heading for Antietam.

Will and Nell had always imagined a house full of children, but it was not to be. She had nearly died giving birth to her only child, and perhaps that is why they cherished him so much.

They had been apprehensive about going to West Point for his passing out parade, mixing with those 'turned-up nose folks' as Will called them, but they wouldn't have missed it for the world. Most of the people that they had met had been so nice and friendly. It didn't surprise them that Elliott was so popular amongst the other newly commissioned officers, though they did experience the odd bit of jealousy from some of the parents who were obviously resentful that Elliott had won the special award for being the top cadet in his intake.

It had come as a bit of a shock when he had written about his plans to become engaged to Eleanor. They had always imagined that he would marry a girl from Traycora. Elliott could have had his pick from at least three of their neighbours' daughters. Will had said that it would be golden-haired Jenny Norris, but Nell had seen how he looked at Dawn Abbott and remembered the way he used give a playful tug at her black ringlets, but the local girls were to be disappointed.

Will and Nell had both been anxious about the trip to Fort Isaac to meet Eleanor and her parents. Nell had agonized over it for weeks before they went. But Will was a modest, almost shy man, and so she had no fear of him speaking out of place and there would be Elliott on hand to guide them through any awkward moments. In the event they had nothing to worry about. Colonel Danvers didn't have a lot to say, but he was polite enough and his wife Elizabeth was a lovely woman and as friendly as can be. Eleanor was more refined than the young girls back home but obviously doted on Elliott, and that was all that mattered. Nell and Will had wanted to send a letter to the Danvers, expressing their sorrow, but it didn't seem right somehow.

3

Once out of the fort, Stanton directed the grey mare towards the main trail, knowing that whichever way he went he was being watched. At least he would cover more distance by keeping to the trail. The surrounding area was rough and rocky and the horse could easily fall, and he would be at the mercy of the pursuing pack that would soon follow him out of the fort.

For the first five minutes or so he continually looked back to see if they intended to give him the start that Nolan had promised. At least the land was open and there was no chance that he was riding into a trap. Elliott had led many patrols through the surrounding countryside and knew the area well. He figured that he had two choices. He could try and reach the river which was at least two hours' ride away, or he could leave the trail when he got to the mountains which were much closer, probably just over an hour away. The decision was made for him when the mare's front legs buckled and he was pitched to the ground. The fall badly winded him as he thudded against the hard ground and he got up gingerly, fearing that he might have broken something.

He tried a few cautious steps and was relieved that he was still able to move quite freely. The horse had also managed to stand up, but Elliott soon discovered that the old mare could not carry him any further. His first impulse was to unsaddle the horse and let it roam free, but he feared that it might find its way back to the fort or be rescued by someone — and the discovery of the horse by his hunters would tell them that he wasn't far away. He decided to leave the trail and head for some woodland about a mile away and hope that he might just make it before his pursuers caught up with him.

He would have to pray that the horse didn't break down again before he reached the cover of the trees. At least the afternoon sun wasn't too hot, which was just as well because he had no water with him or a hat to protect his head. He wondered if he had just been unlucky having the horse go lame like that or perhaps Nolan had deliberately supplied him a suspect mount. If he could reach the woods then he had a plan that might just work, but first he had to get there.

★ ★ ★

Cookie Smithson, or plain Cookie as he was known, made his way to the prison block, wishing that he had passed by the stables for some horse shit to mix in with the grub he had prepared for Stanton. He would have preferred it to have been rat poison, but he couldn't lay his hands on any. Cookie wanted to do something to hit back at Stanton for what he had done to Eleanor Danvers.

She had been a lovely lady who had always been thoughtful and appreciative when he had cooked for the big dinner parties held at the Colonel's house. She had always been nice to him, and not a bit like some of the little bitches that he'd met since he had joined the army. Her ma was a nice lady as well. Some of the officers' wives and daughters acted as though they were royalty, never a please or a thank you, not even a kiss my ass!

Cookie couldn't really understand why they were bothering to feed that bastard, Stanton. Still, he would soon be on his way to the state prison and with a bit of luck he'd get a real going over from some of the inmates once they found out what he'd done. Another thing Cookie couldn't understand was why Captain Pearmain was still so friendly towards Stanton. What with him being a relative to the dead lady. It was probably all about the officer class sticking together, although the others had rightly given Stanton the cold shoulder.

When Cookie arrived at the jailhouse he placed the plate on the steps and beckoned the scruffy, fleabitten dog to sample Stanton's food.

'Go on boy, have a good sniff of that. You can only have a few mouthfuls mind. Must leave some for his lordship,'

The dog sniffed at the pile of beans before walking away without touching them.

'Cheeky bleeder, I cooked those beans myself.'

Cookie opened the door, and it took a moment before what he saw registered. The plate of beans dropped from his hands and crashed to the floor. A pool of blood had formed from the stream that was still flowing from the gaping wound in Sergeant Nolan's throat. Some of the beans floated in the blood like tiny canoes. Cookie vomited and ran outside, without noticing the opened door of Elliott's cell. It would be a long time before he forgot the look on Sergeant Nolan's face.

★   ★   ★

Elliott calculated that it must have been nearly two hours since he had ridden out of the fort and he was puzzled why there was still no sign of his pursuers. He had a clear view of the trail from his position, perched high in one of the tall pines. He was confident that he couldn't be seen and if no one came snooping he might be able to hold up in the woods for a while. It hadn't been easy stabbing the horse with a pointed branch, but he had found the critical point with the first thrust and the animal hadn't suffered too much. Elliott hadn't managed to move quickly enough and the spurt of blood from the animal had squirted into his face. The horse would have been shot or died in the wild, but he still hated having to kill it that way. The actual killing of the animal had been easier than digging the shallow grave to bury it in, using his bare hands and frantic hacking with the sharp point of the branch that he had used to deliver the fatal blow. By the time he'd covered the grave with leaves he was hopeful that it wouldn't be discovered, unless one particular man was with the party who would be hunting him. Elliott knew that there would be no escape from the man no matter how carefully he tried to hide his tracks.

Elliott's thoughts drifted to the time when he got separated from his patrol in Indian country. It was just over a year ago and he'd survived for nearly a week before being rescued by a search party led by David Pearmain. That experience would help in the situation he was in now if he could only outwit his pursuers. He hoped that the party could be fooled into thinking that he'd headed for the river and help his chance of getting clear, but he would need to have lady luck on his side.

4

Cookie Smithson's shouts brought men scurrying towards the prison block, but Cookie was too shocked to tell them what he had seen and could only point in the direction of the horror that had confronted him.

'That bastard Stanton ripped out the Sergeant's throat with the Sergeant's own knife by the look of things,' shouted one of the troopers. 'Let's get after him. There won't be any need for a court this time.'

'What's happened here?' asked the calm voice of Captain Pearmain.

'It's Stanton, sir. He's butchered Sergeant Nolan and escaped.'

'You men need to pull yourselves together,' Pearmain ordered, trying to stop the panic in the men. 'Stanton is probably still inside the fort. Johnson, you go and check with the sentry post and see if anyone left the fort — he may have disguised himself in some way. Corporal Boulton, if Stanton is found then he is to be brought back here and held until I return from reporting this to Colonel Danvers.'

The men dispersed to search the fort, passing on the news to anyone they met and soon the place was a hive of activity. Some men had no intention of delivering him back to Pearmain, at least not alive.

It was almost thirty minutes before Captain Pearmain called off the search inside the fort and assembled eight men to join him on the hunt for Stanton.

'Colonel Danvers wants Stanton to be returned here, alive,' Pearmain instructed, 'but he doesn't expect any of you to endanger your own lives if you make contact with the prisoner.'

* * *

Captain David Pearmain hadn't been too pleased when his uncle had ordered him to take part in the hunt for Stanton. He wanted Stanton arrested, but he had made other plans for the rest of the day and it was inconvenient. If Eleanor had listened to his advice then she would still be alive. He had warned her that there was always trouble when social classes mixed. Stanton might have been an attractive fellow but his father was only a farmer who, according to some, bred hogs. Stanton might be an officer but he had no breeding, no history. Life wasn't all about romance and true love. He hadn't married Eloise for her looks, that was for sure. Such a pretty name, for such an ugly woman. Pearmain was a career soldier and had done well so far, thanks to his father, General Theodore Pearmain using his influence. He enjoyed the military life but he also had a liking for the good life and an eye for the ladies. He had never thought highly of Stanton, even before his association with his cousin began. Stanton was popular with most of the men and the ladies, as borne out by his stupid cousin. But Stanton's courting days were well and truly over now. There would be no going to prison and perhaps being released early on a governor's pardon: Stanton was heading for an execution if he ever he made it back to Fort Isaac alive. Pearmain was thinking that perhaps it wasn't a bad idea after all being responsible for the hunting party, because if they brought Stanton back dead or alive it would be a feather in his cap. He would certainly be in favour with his uncle for avenging the family and it would likely help his promotion prospects as well. He might even get an earlier posting back east, closer to civilization and some fine ladies. It was a pity that he would have to take Eloise with him.

* * *

Stanton had climbed down the tree to stretch his legs to try and stop cramp from developing, but felt vulnerable on the ground so he was soon climbing back up the tree. He had only just settled back in the hideaway-cum-lookout in the tree when he saw the dust clouds in the distance. He couldn't tell how many were in the party or who it was that rode some ten yards ahead of the main group. But the lead rider's identity was soon revealed when he stopped, dismounted and crouched down to inspect the trail. It was Hawky, the man he hoped would not come after him. Hawky, as he had become known, although his Indian name was Great Hawk, was an Indian scout who worked for the army, and there was no one better at picking up a trail. Elliott saw him mount again and point in the direction of the woodland where he was hiding. For a split second Elliott considered climbing down and making a run for it, but he knew it would be futile. He decided to stay put and hope that Hawky would miss something or would be overruled and that the group would ride away, but it was not to be.

As the men drew closer he saw that Captain David Pearmain was leading the party and they were soon entering the woods. One of his pursuers made his intentions clear when he hurled a rope over a branch ready for a lynching. Pearmain would try to stop it, but some of these men were no more than a rabble and would take the law into their own hands when it suited them. Hawky had dismounted and was staring at the spot where the buried horse lay, and Elliott braced himself as the scout let his gaze drift to the base of the tree he was hiding in. He waited for Hawky to look up into the branches and then raise the alarm to signal that he had found his prey. It seemed like an age before Hawky led his horse away from the spot and pointed towards the direction of the river — the same river where Elliott had saved Hawky's life after some soldiers had thrown the Indian into the water during a bout of horseplay. The men hadn't realized that Hawky couldn't swim, and he would have drowned but for Elliott. The scout had just repaid his debt because he surely knew that Elliott was in the woods.

Captain Pearmain lost some of his customary coolness as he scowled at Hawky.

'I hope you haven't lost him,' shouted Pearmain. 'If you have then you'll be looking for another job. I don't see why he would have come into these woods anyway.'

Hawky had experienced the Captain's anger before, but he wasn't frightened by his threats.

'He's been here, sir,' Hawky reported. 'I don't know why but then he headed out of the woods, towards the river.'

Pearmain looked furious as he swung his horse around. 'We'll catch him even if it means running these horses into the ground. Now let's go — and any man who can't keep up had better return to the fort.'

The man who was eager for a

lynching waited for the other riders to go past him before he retrieved the rope and then followed them out of the woods.

Elliott could tell that the men were in an ugly mood and most of them had no intention of escorting him back to the fort. Sergeant Nolan had made it quite clear that he had to escape or die. He was grateful for what Hawky had done, but he couldn't rely upon the scout being so generous next time. With luck he would have a reasonable amount of time before the party gave up the search. He knew it was more risky but he decided that his best plan would be to head back in the direction of the fort, avoiding the main trail. There was a corral to the west of the fort and he would head there and try and steal a horse. He found it more difficult climbing down the tree a second time because of the cramp in his legs. His feet had barely made contact with the soft pine needles when he heard the sound of a pistol being cocked.

'If it isn't the murdering rapist Lieutenant. Now you just turn around nice and slow.'

Elliott turned to see the smiling face of Trooper Luke Bollinger, the man who had thrown the rope over the tree.

'I don't know how you managed to escape, Stanton, but if you try anything with me, you're dead. I was planning to finish you off right here but I like the idea of entering the fort with you as my prisoner.'

'We arrived at Fort Isaac on the same day, Bollinger,' Elliott reminded him. 'Do you really think that I would have done such a thing to my own fiancée or any other woman?'

'I don't give a damn whether you did or didn't, not after what you did today. All I know is that Colonel Danvers is going to be mighty pleased with me when I take you in. Pearmain's following that no-good scout to the river, but I had a hunch you were in these woods so I told them that my horse was lame and I was going back to the fort. I just need to get my mount from back there and then we can get this show on the road.'

As Bollinger slowly edged backwards he repeatedly glanced behind, causing him to trip on a log. Elliott reacted instantly, diving on top of Bollinger and grabbing his wrist in an attempt to wrestle the pistol away from him. Elliott gasped as Bollinger's knee was driven into his groin. The left-hand punch that he delivered into the side of Bollinger's face sent his would-be executioner into a fury and he head-butted Elliott on the bridge of his nose. The sound of the broken bone was like a piece of dry twig being snapped and the blood trickled on to Elliott's lips. Although dazed from the blow, Elliott managed to ram the hand that held the gun against the large fallen log. Bollinger gave an agonized cry and his gun fell to the ground, but he still managed to use the other hand to deliver a blow that caused a gash below Elliott's right cheekbone and left him sprawled in an even more dazed state. Bollinger scrambled to his feet and scanned the area for his gun, unaware that it had been buried beneath the thick carpet of needles as their bodies had rolled about the ground.

'Right, you bastard, I think I'll finish you off right here. Hanging is too good for you. I think I'll just rip open your belly and let you bleed nice and slow. I've heard better men than you scream as they died like you're going to. This one is for Sergeant Nolan.'

Elliott's head was just beginning to clear and the sight of Bollinger holding a large hunting knife came into focus. As Bollinger closed in on him Elliott saw that the hidden branch he'd used to dig the grave for the horse had been exposed during their struggle. Elliott grounded one end of the branch so it formed a spear, which Bollinger impaled himself on as he dived towards him. Elliott rolled to one side and lay exhausted as he listened to Bollinger groaning. It was several minutes before he was able to stand up, and then he pushed Bollinger over on to his back. He had stopped groaning and Elliott Stanton had just killed his first man.

Stanton rested on one knee, still feeling groggy from the blows that he'd taken from Bollinger, and both his cheekbone and nose throbbed. Any hope he had held of clearing his name over the false accusations concerning the rape had gone, now that he had killed a man. It was self-defence but who would believe him. Elliott Stanton was a convicted rapist but he expected to soon become a wanted murderer. He wondered when the nightmare would end.

There would be others just like Bollinger who would want to take the law into their own hands as they sought to dispense their idea of justice and revenge. He thought about his own revenge and of his pride and honour, and his need to track down the animal that had raped his Eleanor and probably tried to kill her as well — the same man who had caused her death and was responsible for the position that he was in now. He found new strength and determination, realizing that for the moment he was a free man. If he was going to die then it would be while he was trying to find the man responsible for all his troubles. He might be a hunted man, but he planned to become a hunter.

★ ★ ★

Bollinger had said that Hawky was leading them towards the river and that meant that he still had some time before they would return to the fort. He would have time to bury Bollinger once he had removed his makeshift burying tool that was still sticking out of Bollinger's chest. He would make a grave close to where the horse was buried.

Before he started digging he located Bollinger's horse, which was close by and secured its reins to a tree.

Searching the saddle-bags he found a pair of civilian pants and a check shirt. They were badly creased but they would attract less attention than his uniform. He quickly changed into the clothes, which were a reasonable fit, and packed away his uniform.

He attempted to clean up his face using some of the water from the canteen on Bollinger's horse. The faintest touch on his nose produced an odd squishy sound caused by broken bone gristle. Bollinger's horse was a powerful-looking sorrel, not as good as his own army horse but it would have plenty of stamina, as did all the horses supplied to the army. He recovered some money from the pockets of Bollinger before he dragged his body towards the spot where he intended to dig the grave. He didn't like the idea of stealing from a dead man, but he would probably have to do lots of things that he didn't like before all this was over. He strapped on the gun belt and civilian pistol that he had also found in

Bollinger's bag. It was against regulations to carry such things and he suspected that Bollinger had been planning to desert. Elliott was pleased about finding the gun because now he wouldn't have to waste time looking for Bollinger's weapon that had been buried beneath the pine needles.

As he raked the earth over the body he wondered if Bollinger had any family. Many of the enlisted men were secretive about their past, mostly because they were running away from the law. It was doubtful if Bollinger was his real name but, whatever it was, Elliott hoped that he wouldn't be missed by his family. By the time he finished smoothing out the ground and had hidden the bloodstained branch there was no trace of what had happened just a short while ago. And providing someone like Hawky didn't come snooping here, then it might stay that way forever.

Elliott rode out of the woods, heading towards a hidden food supply the other side of the fort, knowing that he had some serious thinking to do. His initial thoughts were to lie low until the search for him had eased and it became less risky for him to start searching for the man who had caused him so much grief.

5

Nell Stanton was surprised and anxious when she saw the young officer standing on the porch, and didn't recognize him as one of Elliott's friends that she had been introduced to at West Point. They hadn't heard from Elliott since before the trial, and she prayed that the visitor hadn't come with bad news and hoped that nothing had happened to him in prison.

Lieutenant Everson introduced himself, explaining that he had defended Elliott at his trial. Nell invited Everson into the main room of the house and cleared some sewing off the chair so that he could sit down.

Nell couldn't wait any longer to learn why the Lieutenant had called on them.

'Is it bad news? Has something happened to Elliott,' she asked anxiously.

'Well it's not exactly good news,' Everson replied and then suggested, 'perhaps it would be best if your husband was here so I could tell you together.'

Nell's eyes moistened at the mention of her husband. 'My husband is in the bedroom. He's been very sick for a number of weeks and has lost his speech. It happened just out of the blue and the doctor in town doubts if he'll ever get better. He was such a strong man and now he can't even feed himself or string together more than a couple of words.'

Everson shuffled in his seat and then offered his sympathy before he told Nell that Elliott had escaped from his cell at Fort Isaac some weeks ago and he was still on the run.

The anxiety left Nell; at least her son was alive and perhaps even still free.

'Are they still searching for him, from the fort I mean?' Nell asked.

'The search has been scaled down because the feeling is that he will be a long way from the fort by now. One of the reasons I came was to tell you that they will likely be keeping a watch on your home, figuring that Elliott will try and make it back here.'

'Then they don't know Elliott very well,' said Nell. 'Elliott wouldn't involve us in any of this.'

'He might be worried about you, or might come this way to say his goodbyes if he intends leaving the area, perhaps even heading for the border to cross into Mexico. If he stays in the area then he will eventually be captured and things will be much worse for him.'

'I pray to God that they never catch him,' said Nell, 'even if it means never seeing our son ever again. If there was any justice then Elliott would be a free man and still be in the army, mourning that lovely girl, and he might have caught the real villain by now. And perhaps my husband wouldn't be lying next door having to be fed like a baby. The doctor thinks that his illness was brought on by what happened to Elliott.'

Nell couldn't stop the tears from flowing. She couldn't accept the cruelty of what had happened. She knew that as sure as night followed day, her son was innocent. Elliott had always been a loving and caring boy and he would always be. He had been born good and raised just the same.

Everson could tell that they were kind, generous folks whose lives had revolved around Elliott. The room was littered with photographs of him from a tiny baby to a full grown man. Many of them were of Elliott in uniform and there was an array of cups and medals that he had won at the military academy.

Nell Stanton's face lit up after Everson told her he had uncovered some evidence that would help Elliott in his case concerning the rape of Eleanor.

Everson explained that he couldn't go into the details, and he stressed that it was important that Elliott got in touch with him as soon as possible.

'So there is a chance that Elliott will be proved innocent?' Nell asked, unable to hide her excitement.

'Yes, but I don't want to build your hopes up,' replied Everson. 'It looks as though whoever attacked Eleanor probably came from Fort Isaac.'

'Elliott was convinced that it must have been a stranger who was just passing by,' said Nell.

'There wasn't any evidence to support that view at the time of the trial,' Everson countered.

'But you must feel that he has some sort of chance, Lieutenant,' said Nell, repeating her hope once more, eager to cling on to anything that might end their nightmare.

'There's always hope, Mrs Stanton, but as I said, it is vital that I get in touch with Elliott as soon as possible. He might not want to bring trouble to your door, but he could become a desperate man and if you do see him then you must do your best to get him to give himself up. The longer he is on the run, the worse it will be for him. I'm afraid that his sentence will be reviewed in the light of his escape and unless we can prove his innocence to the original charge his sentence will be increased.'

Everson left the Stanton's house without telling them that their son was in far more serious trouble than they could ever imagine. The chances of Stanton turning up were slim, but he considered that his visit to the Stantons had been worthwhile. Now he could tell Colonel Danvers that he was confident that Stanton was not hiding with his folks. The Stantons were probably nice people, simple folks who lived by standards, loved their fellow human beings, God-fearing people. They were so different to his own parents whose families had made their fortunes by being ruthless and using devious methods. Thinking of his own social class reminded him of the first time that he had met Eleanor at a big social gathering attended by their families. He also remembered how he had begged Eleanor to give up Stanton, reminding her that he wasn't from their class and it would cause problems in the future, but Eleanor was a silly romantic.

Everson had never really loved Eleanor, in fact he hated her after the way that she had embarrassed him by turning down his marriage proposal. She hadn't just turned him down, she had laughed at him, saying how silly they would look walking down the aisle together with him being so much shorter than she was. She had smiled at him when she delivered her final tease and told him that perhaps he could be the little brother that she'd never had. He had vowed that one day he would see that smile wiped off her face.

On the journey back to Fort Isaac, Everson had thought of a way of using his discovery that Will Stanton was a very sick man to help recapture Stanton.

6

Since his escape, Elliott had remained within a narrow ten-mile arc north of the fort, and he was unlikely to encounter any trouble with Indians in this region to add to his woes. He had taken plenty of bully beef and hard biscuits from the hidden army supply and then resealed the boxes. The supply wasn't inspected very often, but he didn't want to have to return to it again because it might be too risky. The cheekbone still throbbed occasionally, but the rest of his wounds had healed and some of the scars were hidden by a heavy beard he now sported. He bore little resemblance to the smartly dressed soldier he had been so recently, but he was reluctant to venture into Jerome, a town just eight miles from Fort Isaac. It was doubtful that anyone would have matched him to the description that had been circulated to the law enforcement agencies, but it was too soon to take the risk. He continued to worry that Hawky would pick his trail again and he had spotted his pursuers more than a dozen times, forcing him to be constantly on the move. Colonel Danvers wouldn't want to give up the search, but there must come a point when the army would have to conclude that he had left the area.

Elliott had vowed to himself that he would somehow prove his innocence. He didn't know how or when it would happen, but he would do it. He might have to go to prison first, but one day the shame that had been brought on his family would be lifted. But for now he would bide his time until he was free to move about and ask questions without arousing suspicion. He prayed that whoever had attacked his Eleanor would not die before he caught him and brought him to justice.

Some men's thirst for revenge might have weakened during the long days and lonely nights, but not Elliott's. The discipline forged by his military training helped him temper his anger with patience. There would come a time when he would need to risk being captured as he ventured into a town, starting with Jerome, in the hope of picking up some clues to the identity of the scum he was after. He had decided that he would wait for twelve weeks before he would put himself at risk, and had devised a simple method of recording each passing week with a notch on a small piece of branch that he kept lodged in his saddle. The day after he had made the eighth mark in the wood he suffered severe stomach pains and developed a temperature. Luckily he hadn't seen any signs of soldiers for over a week and the spot that he was camped in was well secluded.

He had been seriously ill as a boy and nearly died from a bout of fever, but whatever he was suffering from now was ten times worse. As he lay crouched between two rocks he felt the pain in every part of his body, but it was worst of all in his head. It was similar to toothache and alternated between the back of his head and across the temples. He cried out when the pain throbbed from behind his eye sockets. Elliott Stanton was a fighting man but there were times during the first night of his illness when he wished that he would die. By the end of the following day he set off on a walk in a delirious state, not knowing where he was heading but he kept walking, maybe because the pain eased a little. He could hardly see as the light faded and so it didn't matter that he closed his eyes, which seemed to ease the pain as well. The pain disappeared completely when he crashed to the ground and lost consciousness.

★　★　★

When Stanton's delirium finally ended, the pain had eased and apart from his dry mouth, he felt comfortable and for a moment he thought that he must be dreaming. The pillow was soft and there was a fragrance that he hadn't smelt in a long time. When he heard the woman's voice, he really did think that he was dreaming.

'He's awake, Pa,' the voice said. The woman sounded relieved and excited.

'So he is, honey, and that means that you've performed a miracle,' replied Tom Ashley as he smiled at his daughter, Emma. 'I swear that this young feller had at least one foot in the next life. I ain't ever seen anyone so close to death without them dying.'

'I'll get him a drink,' said Emma and hurried across the room to the coffee pot that was brewing on the open fire.

'I'm not sure that he's ready for sitting up just yet, honey, but I expect that his mouth will be as dry as the desert when he fully comes around.'

Elliott could hear the voices but

couldn't make out what they were talking about. He found it difficult to concentrate as he struggled to understand where he might be. Emma had returned with a mug of coffee, the contents of which she had cooled with a generous supply of cold milk. It had been three days since her pa had carried the stranger into their remote farmhouse after finding him wandering around the trail a few miles away. He had been delirious and suffering from some sort of fever and there was an ugly gash across his forehead.

Tom Ashley wasn't sure if the man had been attacked by someone or that he had fallen, but he was still carrying a pistol and his horse was close by. Emma was his only daughter and although only eighteen and a gentle sort of girl, she had nursed the man as well as anyone could have. The stranger might be a no good, but he would get their help until they knew who he was. There was no telling what sort of man was behind that shaggy beard. There hadn't been chance yet to see opened eyes to determine if they were warm or cold. A smile can deceive but not the eyes.

Elliott groaned as he felt a sharp pain from his forehead and he gritted his teeth.

'Welcome back to the land of the living, young feller,' said Tom Ashley.

'Where am I?' Elliott asked, in what was barely a whisper.

'You're in my house, where you've been since I brought you here a few days ago. I'm Tom Ashley and this is my daughter, Emma, who rescued you from death's door, and that's a fact.'

Emma smiled at Elliott but she was still concerned about his condition.

'Don't go asking him lots of questions, Pa. Let him get used to things first.' Emma grabbed the two pillows near the bed and placed them behind Elliott's head to make it easier for him as she helped him drink from the mug. By the time she withdrew the mug from his lips it was empty.

'Thank you,' said Elliott. The voice

was stronger now, just as it was when he continued, 'I can't see. I'm blind. What happened to me?'

Emma Ashley gave her pa an agonized look.

★ ★ ★

Elliott Stanton didn't believe in miracles, even though he had prayed for one often enough during recent months. It had been two weeks since he had found himself in a strange place being nursed by a woman that he could smell and feel, but not see. He had built a mental picture of Emma as she had helped him take short walks around the farm, and he wondered if he would ever get to see the woman who had probably saved his life, although he doubted if it had been worth saving. He had been getting stronger each day, but there had been no improvement to his sight and although an optimist by nature, as the days passed, he was beginning to wonder if he would ever see again.

Without his sight he might just as well have been in prison, and he could forget any chance of clearing his name. As far as Tom and his daughter were concerned, he was just a drifter by the name of Jed Hogan. He had used the name of his uncle just in case his real name was familiar to the Ashleys or any folks that might visit while he was staying there. He hated lying to them but he didn't have much choice unless he wanted to burden them with his story, but most of all he didn't want them getting involved in harbouring an escaped prisoner. He was soon to discover that if Tom Ashley had his way, then he might have no option but tell them the truth. Tom had been pushing for Elliott to be seen by a doctor just in case there was something that could be done to help him with his blindness or at least give him some idea of what might have caused it.

They were finishing their supper when Tom Ashley delivered a suggestion that was to be the cause of a restless night for Elliott.

'I've been thinking about your problem, Jed, and I have an idea that might just help. As I've already told you there ain't any point in you seeing Doc Sloane in Jerome because he's about as useless as they come. He's OK for digging out bullets or hacking off a limb, but your problem is way too complicated for him.'

Emma had just placed a spoon in Elliott's hand and guided it towards the bowl of food, and she was curious to know what her pa had in mind, but she secretly wished that things would stay just as they were. Pa had said that she had saved Jed's life and if necessary she would take care of him for ever. She loved her pa dearly, but her life had taken on a new meaning since Jed had arrived. She knew that Jed liked her and who knows what might happen in time. Of course she really wanted him to regain his sight, but she didn't believe in miracles. They just didn't happen as far as she was concerned.

Tom Ashley had waded through his second helping of pie before he spoke again. 'No, I wouldn't trust Doctor Sloane with one of my mules let alone a human being, but according to a feller that I was talking to in Jerome today there's a real good army doctor over at Fort Isaac. He goes by the name of Simmons and I aim to take you to see him tomorrow, Jed. The fort is a good distance from here being the other side of Jerome, but I was thinking we might go there by wagon first thing in the morning. What do you think?'

Elliott was thinking that Doctor Simmons would easily recognize him even with a beard, but before he could think of something to say, Emma did it for him. 'Pa, how do you know that this army doctor is any better than Doc Sloane? From what you have told me about army doctors most of their work is just doing amputations. Perhaps this doctor won't want to treat civilians and maybe Jed would rather wait to see if nature does its work.'

Tom Ashley stroked his chin before delivering his reply. 'I don't know for sure, honey, just how good this doctor is, but he sounds like a goodun' and I expect he would like the challenge of a complicated case like Jed's. I reckon if nature was going to help then it would have done so by now. Anyway, I ain't going to force Jed into anything he doesn't want to do. How do you feel about it, son?'

'To tell you truth, Tom, I'm willing to try anything and I appreciate that you are trying to help me. But I can also see Miss Emma's point, so if it's all right with you I would like to wait another week before I start putting folks though any trouble on my account. I expect the army doctor is a busy man.'

'It's your call, son, and what you suggest seems like a good idea to me.'

As Emma helped Elliott sip his drink later that night, she could sense that he was troubled and she wanted to help him but didn't know how, except maybe to talk about it.

'Jed, I know it might seem a silly question, but will you be really upset if you never regain your sight? You'll still have your memories and they say people adapt and develop their other senses to cope.'

Emma was sorry that she asked when he replied that he would rather be dead if he could never see again, and that if she didn't mind he would rather not discuss it any more.

* * *

During the following days the proposed trip to the army doctor wasn't mentioned again and he hoped that Tom would forget the idea. Elliott didn't expect any help from nature and had spent many hours trying to decide what to do. There were lots of options but he no longer had just himself and his own folks to consider. He had to think about Tom and Emma and how his arrest would affect them if they were accused of harbouring an escaped prisoner. He decided that if he was going to let Tom Ashley take him to the fort then he would have to tell them the whole truth. If he did that then there was a chance that Tom would forget the idea of taking him in. Then they really would become involved, and he wouldn't allow that to happen.

He was still pondering what to do when the week was up and Tom Ashley asked him if he was ready to go to the fort the following day. Elliott tried to sound enthusiastic about the prospect of the doctor being able to help him. Emma didn't comment this time but he knew that she wasn't pleased about it.

That night it was many hours before Elliott eventually managed to sleep, but at least he had made up his mind and he wouldn't be going to the fort tomorrow. He would tell Tom and Emma the whole story and then he would ask Tom to take him to a quiet spot to allow him to have some time alone. He had decided that while he was alone tomorrow he would end his misery with some honour. He would kill himself.

The next morning it was the familiar sound of Emma preparing breakfast that woke him up and the decision of the previous night came into his thoughts. He felt a strange feeling of relief. There was no shame or guilt because it felt right. He wasn't running away from his problems, just accepting that he was in no position to solve them now. Perhaps he never would have, even had he not become blind, but he would have given it a good try. As he sat up in bed he looked in the direction of Emma and saw the woman who had done so much for him. The shoulder-length hair was dark and not fair as he had imagined. He already knew that she was tall but the figure was fuller than he had pictured it. He smiled as she looked in his direction and held his gaze before she gasped and then ran from the room, not with excitement but in a state of distress. Elliott called after her, realizing why she was so upset but she had no need to be. The large scar that ran from her forehead and down the right cheek didn't alter the fact that to him she was beautiful.

Elliott was up and dressed when Tom Ashley entered the cabin with a broad smile on his face. Tom Ashley was bigger than Elliott had pictured him in his mind and the face was older, lined and weary-looking and not in keeping with such a jovial character.

Tom offered out his hand to Elliott. 'It is true, son, you can see again and you won't be making that trip to the fort after all.'

'I had just about given up ever being able to see again, Tom, and I can't tell you how good it feels, but Emma seems really upset. I think I know why but she has no need to be. She's a lovely-looking young woman.'

'Don't worry, son, she'll come around. I think it was all a bit of a shock for her. She usually wears a scarf when there are folks around, not that it happens very often.'

Elliott wasn't planning on prying into what had happened to Emma, but Tom Ashley told him that an Indian had raked her across the face with a knife when they had raided the ranch. She was only ten years old at the time and had gone to the aid of her ma. Tom had been away and came home to find Emma cradling her dead ma. The scar had faded as she had grown older but Emma was convinced that she was ugly and there was no way of convincing her otherwise. Tom had wanted to move from the area so that Emma could be near some young people, but she begged him to stay. He knew it was because she didn't like mixing with people and it grieved him.

7

During the weeks after Elliott had recovered his sight he was pleased to be able to repay some of the kindness he had received from the Ashleys by helping out around the farm. Tom Ashley was fit for his age and hard-working but there was plenty of work for an extra pair of hands.

It was early one morning when Elliott was called upon to provide some unexpected help. Tom had gone to town on some business and Elliott was just finishing cleaning out the barn when he heard Emma scream. She had brought him a drink earlier and everything had been fine. As Elliott hurried from the barn he heard another scream and suspected that Emma might have seen some sort of creature, a hairy spider or perhaps a small snake.

It was a creature all right, but the two

legged kind who had Emma in a bear hug and was trying to kiss her as she twisted her head from side to side.

'Come on you bitch,' he shouted. 'You should be grateful for a man's attention. I don't expect you get many offers.'

Emma's attacker had been too occupied to hear the advancing steps of Elliott who gripped him by the back of his collar and hurled him to the ground. The man was winded and still dazed as his pistol was lifted from its holster by Elliott who then tossed it some distance away.

Elliott asked Emma if she was all right and if she knew the man.

'I'm just a bit shaken. His name is Jonty Coogan and he used to pester me when I was younger, but pa has told him never to come by here. I suppose he must have seen pa leaving for town earlier.'

Coogan had got to his feet and was weighing up the stranger who had spoilt his chance of having a bit of fun with the woman he had always fancied. She'd filled out some since he'd last seen her and he figured that she would be real hot for it, what with her being out in such a lonely hole as this. He reckoned that he would have been the first that she'd done it with and he always liked that moaning that the first timers usually did. He was never sure what they were moaning and groaning about, fear or pleasure, but it made him feel so good. And now this stranger had ruined it. Perhaps he wanted the ugly bitch for himself, but Coogan wasn't going to give up the chance of having what he'd come for. The feller didn't look anything special. He'd got the better of bigger men than this one so he figured he would give him a beating before he gave Emma Ashley a good seeing to.

Elliott wondered if his strength would hold up if a full-blown fight started with this man. He was also thinking that perhaps it wouldn't be a good idea to get involved and risk attracting too much attention to himself and hoped that the man would just leave.

'I don't take kindly to being hauled off my girl-friend, mister,' Coogan growled. 'Emma and me are what you might call a couple. Ain't that right, honey?'

'We're no such thing,' Emma replied indignantly. 'You had better get out of here before pa gets home. He's only gone to check out the cattle and he'll be back soon.'

Coogan smiled at her. 'We both know that he's heading for town right now and he won't be back in quite awhile. So if your new friend here gets on with cleaning out the hogs or whatever he was doing, you and me can start having some fun.'

Emma was beginning to fear for what might happen to Jed if Coogan turned on him because he still hadn't fully recovered and she doubted if he was ready for brawling.

'Jed here is still recovering from a fever,' explained Emma. 'Now why don't you just leave? I'll promise not to tell pa if you go right now.'

Coogan took a step closer towards Elliott, encouraged by the news that the man who had spoilt his pleasure was probably not up to fighting.

'Now you mention it, he does look a bit shaky, but remember it was him who attacked me and I figure that I should teach him not to poke his nose into another man's business.'

'Leave Jed alone and then we can go inside and perhaps have a talk about us. But I only mean talk, see if we can't be friends,' Emma suggested, trying to humour Coogan.

'Now you're being reasonable, but I can't let this go just like that. I've got a reputation to think about, but as a special favour to you I won't rough him too much.'

Coogan took a wild punch at Elliott who managed to dodge it with ease and then buried his own fist into his attacker's flabby belly. As Coogan fell forward, Elliott head-butted him full on his nose and then delivered a series of blows to the dazed man's head and body. When Coogan collapsed to the ground Elliott started kicking him in a frenzied attack as he lost control. Coogan was no better than whoever had raped Eleanor and Elliott would make sure that he never bothered Emma ever again. He wasn't intent on killing Coogan but he might have done had it not been for the screams of Emma who begged him to stop.

Elliott was shaking as he stepped away from the bloodied Coogan.

'I'm sorry, I'm sorry,' Elliott said to Emma as he realized what he might have done, 'but I don't think he would have been content just to have a friendly chat with you. Men like him will always want to have their way, but I shouldn't have attacked him like that. I guess I just lost control.'

Emma placed a hand on Elliott as she thanked him for what he had done and then started crying as the seriousness of what might have happened to her or Elliott sunk in. Elliott hugged her and he felt the wetness of her tears on his cheek. He brushed the hair away from her eyes and saw her wince, knowing that the cause was once again the scar on her face. He wanted to tell her that she was beautiful and that any man would be happy with her, but the words wouldn't come. Perhaps it was too soon after Eleanor or that he was in no position to get involved with so much trouble hanging over him. He sensed that she was waiting for him to say something to her or even kiss her. He did kiss her on the cheek, but it was a friendly kiss and not the one that both of them craved. Their thoughts were broken by the groaning of Coogan who finally struggled to his feet.

'You bastard, you've broken my nose. You had no need to do that. What harm have I done to you?'

Elliott released Emma and prepared himself in case Coogan wanted to start trouble again but he was confident that the man had no more fight left in him.

'Unless you are really stupid, you'll ride out of here now before Tom gets back and breaks more than your nose,' Elliott advised.

Coogan staggered towards where he had hitched his horse, muttering a variety of threats to Elliott and after a few failed attempts, he eventually climbed on to his animal and rode off.

Elliott promised Emma that he wouldn't tell her pa about what had happened with Coogan, feeling that there was no point in Tom getting into trouble with the law for what he might do to the man. He didn't expect Emma to ever be pestered by Coogan again, but Elliott intended to meet the vile man once more. Jonty Coogan was exactly the type of man that he would be trying to track down, but Elliott would soon discover that he would have no need to go looking for Jonty Coogan.

8

Colonel Danvers had seen much tragedy during his career in the army, the worst cases being of women and children butchered during the height of the Indian troubles. He had also come across the same sort of horrors that some of his own men had inflicted on the Indians. He never ordered the butchery personally but it had happened and it didn't make him feel any better. He was fifty-two years old and he didn't plan to stay in the army much longer. Once all this business with Stanton was over he would start making plans to retire. The death of his daughter had taken its toll. They had been close and he had doted on her. Most men wanted to have a son, but not Danvers, fearing that his own achievements and the many decorations he had received would have put pressure on a son. He had always hoped that a son-in-law would provide him a link with the army, knowing that it was always going to be likely that Eleanor would marry into the military. When Elliott Stanton had asked for her hand in marriage the colonel had been delighted. He liked the man. He was a fine soldier with an extremely bright future. Stanton hadn't come from a military background himself but he was a born soldier. The top brass had already made it clear that he was marked for stardom and the posting to Fort Isaac was just a stepping stone for him.

Danvers had been away visiting another fort on the day of Eleanor's death and Stanton was already in custody when he arrived back. He had listened to his pleas of innocence, not wanting to believe his guilt but knowing that he must have committed the horrible crime. Danvers had met all types of men during his career, including some who would swear on their mother's deathbed to save their own skin.

Stanton was a naturally charming man, but perhaps the charm was all a front that hid his darker, evil side. But why had he found it necessary to commit such an outrage? Was it simply because Eleanor had wanted to keep her purity until they were married in the eyes of the Lord? She would have wanted that because of her upbringing and was entitled to have her wishes respected. None of it made sense, but where passion was concerned, standards and rules meant nothing. Lust could make men behave in strange ways.

He had only hate for Stanton now and would have preferred him to have been executed, but the law demanded otherwise and he would stick by the law. But now that Stanton had managed to escape, murdering Sergeant Nolan in the process, Danvers would get his wish when Stanton was caught and then executed. He was still surprised that

Stanton had managed to outwit such a seasoned campaigner as Sergeant Nolan and he was sorry that he had lost such a reliable soldier.

Danvers had waited three days before the patrol led by his nephew returned, having failed to locate Stanton. It seemed that he had crossed the river and had likely escaped forever, but Stanton was an intelligent man and perhaps a devious one. It was possible that he would be lying low somewhere nearby, planning to make his getaway later. Danvers ordered Captain Pearmain to organize three parties of men and produce a search plan of the area. The parties would commence their search the following day and would continue it for the next month. Hawky was to search alone and report his findings back to Danvers. The news about Bollinger's disappearance gave him some hope that Bollinger might still be on the trail of Stanton. The man had been very close to Nolan and might have deliberately decided to do a solo search, but it was more likely that the man had deserted and like Stanton, would never be seen again.

* * *

As the weeks went by, Danvers had been surprised how well his wife Elizabeth had coped with their daughter's death. She had been so excited about the prospect of her daughter's marriage to Stanton and the thought of having grandchildren one day. They had always planned to have a larger family themselves, but his dedication to his career made them decide otherwise. They hadn't really discussed their loss since Eleanor's funeral, handling the grief in their own way.

A week before the search period would be over and the search parties stood down, Danvers had to spend a night away at Fort Beamont. As well as being commanding officer of Fort Isaac, which was the largest in the area, he was also in overall charge of the smaller forts. He hadn't wanted to go with so much going on, but he was a true professional and duty always came before anything personal.

The time away from Fort Isaac gave him the opportunity to reflect and he decided that he would to take Elizabeth away following the end of the hunt for Stanton. They would have a much-needed holiday back East and make plans for his retirement.

It was almost dark when Danvers reached his quarters and he was surprised to find them in darkness. Elizabeth would be expecting him and it would have been unlike her to be visiting someone at this time of night when he was due home. He lit the oil lamp and it had barely reached its full brightness when he saw his wife slumped in her favourite chair. She was surrounded by Eleanor's dresses, dolls and other items that had belonged to their daughter. He gently prised the book away. It was opened at a page at the top of which read, 'My mummy and daddy by Eleanor Danvers aged seven.' He smiled as he read 'My daddy is in charge of the army and my mummy is the best in the whole world'.

Danvers gently shook his wife's shoulder but there was no response. Elizabeth Danvers had gone to join her daughter. Doctor Simmons told him later that she must have died of a broken heart.

9

Tom Ashley had told Elliott to be prepared to have his breath taken away when he went to do some work in the far meadow and Tom hadn't been exaggerating. Elliott had seen some beautiful sights on his travels but none to match this. It was made the more spectacular by the suddenness of the change. He had been riding a trail though the dense, dark woodland and then the brightness appeared as though a brilliant sun had emerged from behind a black cloud. He dismounted and scanned the valley below. He'd seen waterfalls before but none as high or as wide as the one here. It was some distance away but he could still hear the powerful roar. The pines that wound their way down the other side were staggered in such a way that they might have been planted by man rather than through an act of nature. The terraces in the side of the hill contained wild flowers of almost every imaginable colour. Tom had told him that there were enough tools and materials in the soddy to enable him to fix some of the broken fencing and patch up the soddy. As his horse took its first tentative step on the winding path to the valley below, Elliott pulled him to a stop and dismounted, deciding to walk through the path and take in the scenery. He hitched the animal in the shade of the trees and then unfastened the small parcel of food that Emma had prepared for him. Tom reckoned that the job would probably take three or four hours and Emma planned to visit him if she finished her chores in good time.

★ ★ ★

By the time that Elliott made his way back up the trail to where he'd left his horse it was mid-afternoon and the job had taken longer than expected. He was disappointed that Emma hadn't visited him because it would have been good to have talked to her away from the house. He would have found it easier to try and reassure her about her scar, which he sensed was still troubling her, and perhaps he could have hinted about some of his own problems that he needed to sort out. As he reached the top of the climb he was slightly breathless, but he was getting stronger and fitter with each passing day. He was tying the food bag to the sorrel when he noticed the opened saddle-bag at the same time as he heard a weapon being cocked.

'Unbuckle that belt as slow as you can, mister, or you'll die right here.'

'Don't try anything foolish,' advised a second voice.

Elliott let the belt fall to the ground, cursing himself for being caught off guard, perhaps lulled into a false sense of security by the peacefulness of the surroundings.

He followed the next order and

slowly turned to face the two men. One of them was Jonty Coogan and his face was still bruised from the beating that Elliott had given him a few weeks earlier.

'I think we have a little score to settle with you,' said the other man, 'for what you did to my brother Jonty, and just because he was sweet-talking that man-hungry Ashley woman. Most women want it but try to play hard to get so it gets the man extra horny.'

'Emma Ashley didn't want anything to do with this excuse for a man here,' snapped Elliott, feeling himself getting riled up and forgetting the odds were against him.

'What did I tell you, Luke? This feller is downright insultin',' said Jonty.

'He just needs teachin' a lesson,' said Luke Coogan, 'that he can't poke his nose into other folks' business — and the lesson is about to start.'

Luke Coogan raised his gun, and although Elliott moved away from the blow it still caught him on the side of the face and sent him sprawling against the sorrel before he fell to the ground.

'Don't just stand there, kick him and kick him hard,' Luke ordered his brother. Jonty may have been slow on the uptake but he made up for it as he repeatedly kicked Elliott until he lost consciousness.

'That's enough, Jonty,' Luke shouted. 'I think you've paid him back and he ain't any good to us dead. Let's tie him up and then strap him to his horse.'

When Elliott opened his eyes he was facing the ground and the blood from his nose was dripping onto the side of his horse. His eyes felt as though they were coming out of their sockets. His head throbbed and he gasped with the pain from his ribs as they pressed against the hard saddle. He had no idea where they were heading or how long they had been on the move.

'It looks as though Sleeping Beauty is awake, Jonty. I thought we might have reached Fort Isaac before he came to.

That nose of his has been running like a tap.'

Elliott hadn't expected that his days on the run would end like this. That he would be 'arrested' by two halfwits. He was puzzled how they could have discovered who he was. There was no way that they would have recognized him from the posters that he was certain would have been displayed in the towns across the territory. He had expected that it wouldn't have been long before a professional bounty hunter would have come after him for the reward, but now it would go to the Coogans. How ironic it would be if he was recaptured by accident. At least the fact that they were taking him back to the fort proved that Jonty Coogan hadn't been involved in the attack on Eleanor. Even Coogan wouldn't have been silly enough to risk going so close to the scene of the crime.

Luke Coogan helped solve the mystery of his 'arrest' when he explained, 'In case you're wondering why we're taking you the fort, well we had a little look in your saddle-bag and saw those army bits and pieces so we reckon that you're a deserter.'

'I was in the army once but I'm not a deserter,' Elliott replied. 'Those things that you found in my saddle-bag are just keepsakes.' Elliott hoped that all was not lost if he could just convince them that there would be no reward.

'So that means you must have stolen them things, so we reckon the army will reward us for handing over a thief. Stealing government property is a very serious offence,' said Jonty.

'You'll be wasting your time and the army's,' replied Elliott.

'Anyways, we ain't arguing with you,' growled Luke Coogan. 'We're taking you to Fort Isaac and we'll take our chances on getting some sort of reward. Thanks to you interfering over that Ashley bitch, our ma threw Jonty out of the house. So we're heading for Wenlow Creek and Fort Isaac is on the way there.'

Elliott didn't know how the news about Jonty's assault on Emma had got to their mother, unless perhaps Jonty had been bragging about it to his brother.

Elliott was glad that they had stopped and let him ride upright, and the blood was no longer leaking from his nose. Elliott calculated that they must be about six miles from the fort, and once they were out of the wooded area it would be a straight flat trail. The Ashleys would think badly of him for leaving without any explanation, being unaware of what had happened to him. He had enjoyed the short time that he had been with them and he owed them his life, for what it was worth. He felt sad that he would probably never see Emma again, never have the chance to tell her how he really felt about her: that he loved her just as much as he had the woman that had been robbed from him. He'd hoped that they would never find out who he really was. He tasted the fresh blood in his mouth and feared that the kicking had done some internal damage to his organs. He began to feel faint due to the amount of blood that he had lost. He was so weak that he barely reacted to the sound of a shot that hit a tree close by.

'Stop right there and throw down your weapons,' someone called out from behind the rocks near the trail, 'or I'll kill you both and I don't mind which it is.'

'Jesus Christ, Luke. Who can it be?' Jonty asked his brother.

'Just do as he says,' ordered Luke as he drew his pistol and dropped it to the ground. Jonty hadn't really needed his brother's order and his weapon dropped onto the soft soil.

'What do you want, mister?' Luke shouted out as he and his brother looked to see who had fired at them. 'We ain't got any money. We're just on our way to Fort Isaac with this here deserter.'

'I've been trailing that man you've got there for weeks,' was the reply from the hidden man. 'He's a wanted man and he's mine. Now ride out of here.'

'But the — ' Jonty started to protest but his brother cut him short.

'Just do as he says.'

The voice sounded vaguely familiar to Elliott but he'd never met any bounty hunters before. It didn't really matter to him who it was; nothing had changed apart from his captor.

Another shot splintered the same tree and the Coogans urged their mounts forward as though it was the start of a race. It seemed like several minutes to Elliott before the mystery man approached him and his face came into focus.

'Let me get you down from there, Lieutenant, and make you more comfortable.'

'Hawky!' Elliott whispered as he recognized him. 'I thought the voice was familiar but I had no idea it was you. I guess you've come to turn me in this time. I know you led the hunting party away from me in the woods.'

'I'm not going to turn you in, Lieutenant, even if you are wanted for murder. I'm here to bring you a message, but let's get you down from that horse, give you something to drink and clean you up.'

Elliott first sipped and then gulped the water from the canteen and in just a few minutes he felt better as Hawky bathed his wounds and bound his ribs.

'I've been looking for you to pass on a message about your father, and its not good news.'

Hawky explained to him that Lieutenant Everson wanted him to know that his father was very sick and asked Hawky to find him and pass on the message. Elliott was grateful to Hawky for putting himself at risk once more by delivering the message. There was always the chance that the army would have someone staking out his folk's place, but he would just have to take his chances.

10

Hawky had explained that he had been looking for him for over a week when he had stumbled on him and the Coogans by chance. He wasn't sure who it was strapped to the sorrel at first but he thought Bollinger's horse was familiar and then he had spotted the army brand on it. Hawky knew that it wasn't Bollinger and although Elliott's hair had grown, the thick curls were quite distinctive.

When Hawky and Elliott reached the main trail they could see Fort Isaac in the distance and Elliott pulled up his horse. It was time to bid farewell to a man that he was proud to call his friend.

'This is as far as you go, Hawky. I'll never forget what you've done for me.'

Before the two men separated, Elliott told Hawky about the Ashleys and of his plans to return to their place and asked him to call on him there in a few weeks time. As Elliott watched Hawky ride away he remembered that he had meant to ask him how and when they had found Bollinger's body.

It would take two days of hard riding to reach home and he had taken a route that skirted well away from Fort Isaac to reduce the risk. Hawky had given him some food so that he would not have to acquire some on the journey. He hadn't planned to stop at any towns on the way but when he saw the signpost to Jerome, he had second thoughts and reminded himself of the dangers in going back to his home where there was a real chance that he would be recaptured. He would still go and see his pa, but first he would visit Jerome and see if he could find out anything that might help trace the man he was after. This might be his one and only chance and he decided to take it.

★ ★ ★

It was mid-morning when Elliott rode into Jerome, a town he had only visited once before and there was little chance that he would be recognized by any of the locals — not now that he looked so much like a typical saddle bum that even his own ma would struggle to recognize him. He wondered whether he should use the name of Jed Hogan because there might be a chance that Tom Ashley might have mentioned him during his visits to town, but thought it unlikely. He had waited months for this time to come when he would start his search for the man he wanted to help clear his name and now he felt a mixture of excitement and tension. He had always known that he was going to need a large slice of luck to find his prey, but at least he was about to do something and he felt good about it. There was always the chance that the man might come from Jerome or perhaps be working nearby and frequented the town. Some men would blab about anything when they were full of liquor and might even admit to raping a woman when their tongue was loose.

Elliott's first call was to the local store to buy some fresh clothes and boots and a supply of tobacco. The old timer in the store pointed out that the barber also had a bath on the premises. Elliott took the hint and that was his next port of call. He skipped the offer of a shave but had the hair lightly trimmed, and the bath that followed was pure luxury.

'It's time you were out of there, feller,' the barber shouted, and brought an end to Elliott's brief moment of relaxation. He rebound his ribs and changed into his new clothes.

'Are you sure I can't shave off that shaggy mess?' the barber asked. 'There might just be a handsome young face under there but the girls wouldn't know.'

Elliott smiled at the old timer. 'No thanks, but I certainly enjoyed the soak in the tub. I'd appreciate being able to leave these old clothes if you wouldn't mind disposing of them.'

'Sure thing, just leave them there.'

He left the barber's shop feeling that he had handled his first contact reasonably well, and he was about to cross the street to the Jerome Palace saloon when he spotted the two men in uniform. They didn't look familiar, but there was no point in taking a chance so he waited until they were some distance away before he moved on.

The first beer that he ordered at the Palace hadn't had time to settle before his glass was empty. He had never been a lover of liquor but it tasted so much better than it had ever done before.

'You looked as though that was your first drink in a while,' said the barman as he took the glass away. 'I guess you'll want another.'

Elliott nodded to indicate that he would. 'It has been quite a long time since I had the pleasure of a drink.'

'And what about a woman?' asked the bartender. 'I bet you haven't been with a warm-bodied woman in a while either.'

Elliott was taken back by such a personal question but thought it best to humour the man.

'You would win your bet but a good drink is my first priority.'

The bartender smiled and winked at Elliott. 'It wouldn't be if you saw the girls that Miss Shelley has upstairs. Would you be interested?'

'I sure would,' replied Elliott, who had just thought of an idea that might help him, 'but it would have to be one that's used to a bit of roughness, if you know what I mean. It's been quite a long time and I've got some making up to do.'

The barman smiled. 'Then you'll want Angie. She's the one for you, providing you don't mind them big, in all the right places of course. She's what you might call a sight for sore eyes.'

'She sounds interesting,' said Elliott trying to sound enthusiastic.

'Well, I happen to know that she's

free, so when you finish your beer, head up those stairs and you'll find her in the third room on the left. Make sure that you say that Frank sent you up, so that I'll get my commission and you'll get charged a fair price.'

Five minutes later Elliott was standing in a room watching the naked body of the biggest woman that he had ever seen. He hadn't heard a woman snore before, nor had he ever heard a man snore quite as loud as Angie did at this moment. He was within a step of escaping out of the door, when she called out.

'I hope you're not thinking of running out on the prettiest girl in Jerome just because she was catching some beauty sleep. That last cowboy was so horny that he just left me exhausted but I'm ready to go again, if you are, honey.'

'I didn't want to disturb you, miss. By the way, Frank sent me.'

'Good, Frank usually sets me up with the sort of men that I like and I like you cowboy. Come and make yourself comfortable.'

Elliott sat on the edge of the bed and at close quarter Angie was a pretty woman. He guessed that she was no more than twenty-three. Those big green eyes and smooth skin were the highlight of a face that bore none of the hallmarks of the hard profession that she was in. The blonde hair was shoulder length and pretty. It was difficult to avoid looking at her breasts, which must have been close to twice the size of a normal well-endowed woman.

'You're making me feel overdressed, cowboy. Why don't I just help you off with some of these clothes after you've taken that piece of iron off? One of the other girls got herself shot in the leg only last week because some damn fool left his gun strapped to his leg while he was trying to perform.'

It wasn't going to be easy explaining to Angie that he wasn't interested in performing with her or anyone else. 'I don't mean to offend you, Angie, but

I'm not here for business. I'll pay you of course but I just want to talk.'

Angie raised her eyebrows and sighed. 'I don't believe it! There I was praising Frank just now and he's gone and sent me up a dud. Look, if it's your first time or you're worried about catching something off me then there's no need to worry. You won't be scratching when you leave here, not unless you are already.'

'No, it's nothing like that. When I say that I want to talk I really mean that I'm looking for some information.'

Angie shook her head. 'No, no, no! I'm sorry, handsome, but I don't talk to lawmen and I don't talk about a man who has shared this bed with me. What happens between these sheets stays private.'

Elliott had planned to avoid telling her why he was really there but Angie was obviously a sharp lady and he decided that it would be best to tell her the truth or at least some of it.

'I'm looking for the man who raped

my girlfriend about ten miles from here some months back. It happened near Fort Isaac and I was hoping that you might have heard some loose talk.'

'I'm sorry, honey. You seem a genuine sort to me, so I guess you are telling the truth, but I don't think I can help you. I get to see just about every sort of man there is and some of them cut up a bit rough at times. I don't doubt that some of them fantasize about raping me while they're doing it but I can't say I know anyone that I could call a rapist. Sorry.'

Elliott thanked her and pulled out a ten dollar bill from his pocket and handed it over. 'Is that enough?'

'Sure, that's plenty, honey. Look, I can ask around the other girls and if I find out anything then I'll leave a message for you with Frank and then you can call up and see me.'

When Elliott reached the door she called after him. 'I hope your girl gets over it, honey.'

Elliott replied with a simple thanks

and she couldn't see the hurt on his face.

As Elliott was leaving the bar, Frank the bartender made a wisecrack and he gave him a smile in return before he pushed open the swing doors and walked outside. He would try his luck at Jerome's other saloon across the street.

The bar looked a lot rougher than the previous one and he doubted if any girls would be doing business here. He downed his first beer as though it was the first one of the day and the conversation followed along similar lines as to the one with the previous barman.

'You sure are thirsty, stranger.'

'I've been looking for work and done some hard riding for the last three days.'

'There's not much work around these parts, unless you want to try your hand at being a deputy sheriff.'

Elliott gave a wry smile. 'I'm more of a farming man and never been much good with a gun or brawling, as you can probably see from the state of my nose.'

'Well that's a pity, friend, because the deputy got himself killed last week and the sheriff is on the lookout for a replacement. If you plan to stay around until tomorrow you'll get to see the hanging of the feller that shot the deputy.'

The mention of hanging reminded Elliott of his own position and he tensed up. A thin, weasel-faced man at the end of the bar had been staring at him and it made him feel uneasy.

'Talking of hanging,' said one of the group sitting at a table near the bar playing cards, 'a trooper was telling me last week that they still haven't found that rat who raped the Colonel's daughter and murdered a soldier.'

'They'll catch him soon,' replied the barman. 'That Colonel ain't gonna' call off the hunt. When I first heard about what had happened out there, I thought young Clint had been up to his tricks again.'

The barman had addressed his remarks to the men playing cards: Jim Slater, the storekeeper, John Cluger the town's blacksmith and Silas Jenson who owned the saloon.

Jim Slater frowned at the mention of Clint Makin. 'He gives me the creeps that boy. I had to chase him out of the store only yesterday after I caught him giving my Mary one of those funny stares.'

'No harm in just staring, Jim,' the blacksmith said.

'Perhaps he was just admiring a fine-looking woman.' Cluger winked at Silas Jenson. Mary Slater was many things, but pretty wasn't one of them. She was almost as wide as she was tall and Slater was only playing cards because she had ordered him to get out from under her feet.

'I knows she's pretty,' replied Slater, taking Cluger's comments seriously, 'but she's old enough to be his ma.'

'My old pa always said that it wasn't a good idea to marry a pretty woman,' said Jenson.

'That sounds like strange advice to me,' said Slater, still unaware that his two companions were teasing him. 'What were his reasons?'

'He figured that a good-looking wife will always attract a lot of attention from other men. And unless you can keep her happy all the time she'll end up being unfaithful.'

'If a man neglects his wife then it's his own fault,' added Slater.

Elliott was finding the men's conversation amusing but he wished they had said more about the man who obviously pestered women.

The little feller at the end of the bar was beginning to annoy him and Elliott stared him out, but didn't feel any better when the man took a final swig of his drink and left.

The barman shook his head as he watched the little man hurry towards the door. 'I wonder what Eli is up to, hurrying off like that.'

'He'll be off to see his mate, the

sheriff,' said Jenson. 'He's been trying to impress the sheriff in the hope of getting the deputy's job. Can you imagine the little feller being a lawman?' The three card players laughed at the suggestion and it took a while before they settled back into their game.

Elliott's instinct was to get out of town as quickly as possible but the conversation at the card table held his attention.

'I still say that Clint Makin is harmless,' said Jenson, picking up the conversation about the town weirdo. 'It's his brother Seth who is the real woman chaser, or at least he was.'

'I'll second that,' added Cluger. 'I reckon some of the things that Clint got blamed for were done by Seth. He takes after his pa when it comes to women. Some say that they fathered more than a dozen children between them and most of them have different mothers.'

'Some of those kids may not know that Seth is their pa, but come tomorrow it won't matter none because he'll be dead.'

Elliott stared straight ahead as he heard the saloon doors swing open, and his worst fear came true when he heard one of the men at the card table greet the sheriff. 'That's him, Sheriff,' shouted Eli. 'You wait and see when he turns around.'

Elliott tried to remain calm, ignoring the fact that he was the subject of Eli's comments but the sheriff was soon by his side.

'Do you mind turning around, stranger?'

Elliott turned to face the lawman. 'Is there some kind of a problem, Sheriff. I'm just minding my own business, having a quiet drink.'

The sheriff stared into Elliott's face and then at the Wanted poster that he had unfolded.

'I think you're right, Eli. Its either him or his double. There's no point asking him his name.'

Elliott was annoyed with himself for

not following his hunch about the man they called Eli and ridden out of town before the sheriff arrived.

Sheriff Ned Tatum dropped the poster and drew his gun at a commendable speed for a man who must have been close to sixty years of age, or else he had witnessed some hard times. He dwarfed Eli who was grinning like a schoolboy, eager to be rewarded for some good deed. The sheriff whipped Elliott's gun from its holster and tucked it into his own belt.

Elliott had seen the name of Johnny Short on the Wanted poster and was relieved that it confirmed that they had not recognized him as Elliott Stanton. He hoped to be able to bluff his way out of the trouble that he was in. 'I think there's been some mistake here, Sheriff. I haven't done anything wrong. My name is Jed Hogan and I have never broken the law in my life.'

'That's what you call yourself today, but I expect that you've had more names than a saloon girl's had men in her bed.'

'He seems like a nice enough feller to me, Sheriff,' said the barman. 'He's only here looking for some work.'

'You might be right, Charlie, but he might also be the man who's wanted for killing at least two men and maybe more. Either way he's heading for one of my cells.'

Elliott didn't see any point in protesting further as the sheriff ordered him to head for the door and cross the street to the sheriff's office.

Jerome was a medium-sized town and with two saloons it meant that there was always the chance of trouble, which was why the sheriff's office contained three large cells. Elliott had never been inside such a place before and the first thing that struck him was the foul smell.

'There's only one other guest in here at the moment,' explained the sheriff, 'but Mr Seth Makin will be leaving us tomorrow and he won't be going to

115

where the angels are.'

Elliott was led to the middle of the three cells, but there was no sign of life from the other cells and he didn't get a glimpse of the man he was now very interested in.

'Eli will bring you some grub later and he'll empty that pot in the morning. I'm going over the road to send a telegraph message to Marshal Clayton. He should be here in a couple of days to collect you unless you really are telling the truth and you have a double.'

Elliott surveyed his miserable surroundings and noticed the pot whose contents had almost reached the top. The blanket that covered the bed was badly stained and he wondered how many men had used it since it was last washed. That's if it had ever been washed. After he heard the sheriff leave the office he took the blanket and shook it against the bars of the cell and then folded it before placing it back on the bed as a form of cushion. As he sat reflecting on the new mess that he was in he heard the sound of snoring from the next cell. Of all the things that he had imagined could have happened to him by venturing into the town, he had never expected to be the victim of mistaken identity.

It was almost dark when the sheriff and Eli returned to the office. The sheriff pointed a rifle at him while Eli opened the cell and passed him a plate of food and a mug of almost cold coffee. The food looked quite reasonable and there was plenty of it.

'I don't know how long you'll be with us, Short, but you won't starve while you're here, I promise you that.'

Elliott was on the verge of protesting again that his name wasn't Short, but decided against it. It had already occurred to him that there might come a point when he would have to decide whether to tell the sheriff the truth about himself. It might be a case of being hung in the name of Johnny Short or executed for the killing of

Bollinger. The way things stood he would opt for hanging as Short because it would save his folks some grief and further shame. If they never heard from him again then they would think that he was probably safe somewhere far away. So he decided that he wouldn't reveal his true identity even if it meant that he would hang.

Eli locked the cell door and moved towards the next cell.

'Wakey, wakey,' Sheriff Tatum roared into Makin's cell.

Judging by the grunting and swearing Elliott guessed that the man in the next cell might have preferred to have remained asleep.

'You've got some company next door, Makin. He says his name is Hogan but he's more likely to be a wanted gunslinger by the name of Johnny Short and a murderer just like you, but I don't expect he's as evil as you are.'

Makin had either drifted back to sleep or was uninterested because he didn't comment on the sheriff's remarks.

Elliott had eaten half the food when the sheriff appeared in front of his cell door again.

'Don't go feeling sorry for that scum next door just because he's ready for hanging. He's as sly as they come and just as mean. He shot my deputy through the eye as he lay on the ground after he was caught trying to rape the deputy's wife.'

The sheriff left the area of the cells and when the slurping and belching had stopped, Makin called out. 'Hey, Hogan! Are they going to hang you tomorrow as well?'

Elliott didn't really want to engage in conversation with Makin, but after what he had heard about him over at the saloon and just repeated by the sheriff it was possible that he was the man that he was looking for. He realized that he might be clutching at straws but there must only be a small number of men who would stoop to such a hideous crime of raping a woman. Perhaps fate had been kind to him and brought him to the very man that he was after, even though at this stage he wasn't sure how it would help him, given his present circumstances.

For the moment Elliott would humour the despicable character in the next cell.

'No, I'll only be here until the Marshal arrives and then they'll realize that I'm not this Johnny Short and there's been a mistake.'

'Yeah, mistaken identity,' said Makin. 'It's happened to me a couple of times but it won't help you none. Marshal Clinton will likely shoot you on the way back and claim the reward. I hear that he's a real evil bastard and just uses the law to suit himself. Hey, I don't suppose you've got any baccy?'

Elliott still had a full pouch from his earlier purchase at the store and he threw the baccy in the direction of the next cell. The baccy was grabbed from where it had landed in front of Makin's cell but there was no offer of thanks.

Makin didn't bother to speak after he

had fired up his first cigarette and Elliott had once again been mulling over events and questioning why life had dealt him such a cruel hand. He was on the verge of sleep, despite the hardness of the bed and the roughness of the soiled blanket, when Makin called out.

'Are you awake, Hogan?'

Elliott was of a mind to remain silent, not really feeling in the mood to make any conversation, but after a delay he answered, 'Almost. Do you want to talk?'

'Not really, I was just wondering, that's all.'

Elliott struggled to get to sleep after the interruption and tried to engage Makin in conversation again. 'Makin, are you frightened of dying?' Elliott asked and before Makin could reply, added, 'I guess all men are when they know its going to happen.'

'Well I ain't,' Makin growled. 'I've lived my life the way that I wanted to. Lived it to the full some would say. I've had my share of fun and more women than most and given them pleasure at the same time, even though some of them played hard to get.'

The last remark struck a cord with Elliott. 'What, you mean that you forced yourself on some women?'

'I gave them what they really wanted but maybe they was too frightened to admit it. You know, the sort of women who have been preached to that it's wrong. So they put up a bit of a struggle to ease their guilt.'

'You seem to have a twisted view of womenfolk, Makin. In my experience most women are gentle creatures and not at all like you describe.'

'Then you haven't met many real women, is all I can say. I wouldn't be facing a hanging tomorrow if it wasn't for a woman. Josie Daniels was all over me until she heard her damned husband coming and then she cries rape and I ended up plugging her husband. Now she's a widow and I'm due for a hanging.'

Elliott didn't see any point in getting into a discussion about morality with a man who would be dead by this time tomorrow, but he couldn't ignore the fact that the Makin could be the man he was after. If Elliott could only link Makin to Eleanor's rape then he would be able to clear his name. He was confident that if this happened then he could plead self-defence for the killing of Bollinger. He might have been feeling quite different had it not been for the misunderstanding when he had been talking to Hawky. Elliott was under the misapprehension that Bolllinger's body had been found and unaware that he was wanted for the murder of Sergeant Nolan.

11

Sheriff Tatum had been up for nearly two hours by the time he made his way to the telegraph office. He would preside over his eleventh hanging today and wasn't looking forward to it, even though the man had killed his best friend. At least he need have no worries about hanging the wrong man. But Tatum was concerned about the other man that he had arrested believing him to be Johnny Short. There was something about the man that bothered Tatum, who considered himself to be a good judge of character and able to spot a troublemaker quicker than most men. During his long years as a lawman this attribute had proven an asset and it had often enabled him to stop trouble starting. Tatum consoled himself by thinking that no real harm would be done if the man he was holding wasn't

Johnny Short. The Marshal would be a mite annoyed about travelling the fifty odd miles from Millcrae to Jerome but that couldn't be helped. As for the man himself, he was getting well fed and he didn't seem in a hurry to do anything special. If he really was just a drifter a couple of days in a cell wouldn't do him any harm.

* * *

The sheriff had just reached the entrance to the telegraph office when he was joined by Eli. The little man was a willing enough sort, but he wouldn't make a deputy in a month of Sundays. He was too jumpy by far and most folks couldn't abide him, and they certainly wouldn't respect him.

'Morning, Sheriff. It looks like it's going to be dry for the hanging. Do you reckon many folks will turn up?'

'I'm sure there'll be a lot of morbid onlookers come noon time as well as the many friends that Carl Daniels had.

He was a popular man and I for one will miss him. I take it that everything is quiet over there?'

'Sure thing, Sheriff. Makin is snoring as usual and that Hogan feller is just staring at the ceiling. Do you think Marshal Clinton will get here soon?'

'I hope to find out in just a couple of minutes,' replied Tatum as he pushed open the door to the telegraph office.

Bill Mason exchanged greetings with the sheriff but ignored Eli as he unclipped the slip of paper and handed it to the lawman.

'I just knew it, I just knew it,' the sheriff repeated.

'Is it from the Marshal, Sheriff?' Eli asked.

'It is but it's not good news — well it is for one man. Eli, you had better get over to my office and release that young feller we arrested yesterday. Tell him that I'm sorry and that'll I'll buy him a breakfast at Tony's place.'

Eli looked surprised and couldn't quite take in his instructions.

'You mean that you want me to release that killer?'

'I can't remember what that feller said his name was but it isn't Johnny Short, and that's a fact.'

'But how can you be sure, Sheriff?' asked a disbelieving Eli, 'when he looks so much like the man on the Wanted poster.'

'On account of the fact that according to this here message from the Marshal, he shot Johnny Short dead just two days ago, that's why. Now get over to the cells and let him out. I've got to see a few people about the hanging. You had better stop by Tony's and explain that the young feller's breakfast is on me.'

Eli was clearly disappointed by the news about Hogan not being the man that he had alerted the sheriff to. It meant that he had lost his share of the reward and of improving his chances of becoming a deputy. He still reckoned that the man was a villain, whoever he was, but he'd been told to let him go and that is what he would do.

Elliott was doing some exercises in his cell when Eli came into the jail, and he became puzzled when he saw Eli wrestle with the bunch of keys and then unlock his cell door. There was no sign of the sheriff and it seemed odd that the little man would risk being overpowered, especially as his gun remained in its holster.

'You're leaving, Hogan, or whatever your name is,' Eli snapped. 'I mean you are free to go. The sheriff said to tell you that there's been some mistake and he's sorry. If you're interested he'll buy you a breakfast at Tony's place across the street.'

Elliott was shocked by the news but for the moment uncertain as to what to do. He would be glad to get away from the stench and he wouldn't have to worry about the marshal getting up to his tricks and claiming a false reward, but he didn't know what to do about Makin. He had planned to ask Makin directly if he had raped Eleanor, just before he was being led away for the hanging, and hope that he would confess what he had done to the sheriff. After all, Makin had nothing to lose. Sometimes even the most violent and ruthless men can change when they are close to the end, and have the fear of death and the uncertainty of whether they are heading for some final reckoning. If Elliott had known Makin longer then he would have realized that he wasn't such a man. Elliott was normally cool under pressure but he suddenly saw Makin as being the one man who might be able to help him, but he needed to keep Makin alive for that. He would need to act quickly before the sheriff came back.

Makin could see Eli hand over the gun and belt to Elliott. 'Hey, friend,' Makin shouted. 'I hope you'll be there to say goodbye to me at noon.'

Makin was ready to make another wisecrack when he saw Elliott draw his gun and point it at Eli. He couldn't hear what the feller had said to the sheriff's lapdog but he was sure interested when he saw him remove the gun from Eli's holster and throw it into the locked cell.

* * *

Elliot kept the gun pointing at Eli as he looked out of the window, fearing that the sheriff might return. He had noted the welcome sight of two horses tied to the hitch-rail across the street. So far so good, he thought as his heart pounded.

Elliott was committed now. There was no going back and he forced himself to take control as he faced Eli. 'Right, do exactly what I tell you and I promise that you'll come to no harm. I'm no friend of Makin but I need him to help clear my name. Make sure you tell the sheriff that. Now open up Makin's cell and let him out.'

Eli's face had turned pale with fear and he struggled to open the cell, not really believing the promise that he had just been given about his own safety.

Makin had not heard what Hogan had said to Eli and he whooped with delight as he came out of the cell.

'I owe you one for this, stranger. I ain't ever been that close to dying before and I guess the angels are looking after me.' Makin sniggered and then turned towards Eli. 'And I guess I owe you one as well, you little runt.'

Eli backed away and looked towards Stanton, hoping for protection.

'We need to get moving,' Elliott snapped. 'See if you can find anything to tie this man up with. Once he's secured we can make a dash for the horses across the street.'

'Aye aye, Captain,' replied Makin sarcastically. He didn't take kindly to orders from anyone, not even someone who had probably saved his life.

A quick search of the office failed to find any rope and Elliott told Makin to rip up one of the blankets from the cell. Makin set about tearing the blanket into strips, as though it were paper, and then bundled Eli into the sheriff's chair.

Elliott again watched anxiously out of the window as Makin pulled the strips of material as tight as he could, enjoying the discomfort that he was causing the little man. Makin tied the final piece of blanket around Eli's mouth to stop him from yelling for help.

'I bet you wished you'd cleaned those blankets more often now. I reckon this blanket has been pissed on often enough,' Makin said and roared with laughter.

'Where's my gun?' Makin stupidly asked the fully-gagged Eli. The shrug of the shoulders earned Eli a vicious blow to his face and the strip of blanket was soon dampened with blood. Elliott was beginning to have some doubts as to whether he was doing the right thing. Makin was just about the meanest-looking man he had ever seen and one of the biggest as well.

'Let's go, now,' shouted Elliott, eager to prevent Makin from getting a weapon. He headed for the door and

Makin followed, but as Elliott started his run across the street, Makin turned back towards the office.

'I ain't leaving that baccy behind,' he shouted back to Elliott.

Elliott carried on running and had mounted his horse before Makin emerged from the office clutching the tobacco pouch. Makin moved remarkably quickly for a big man and he was soon mounting the horse. The killer and his unlikely rescuer galloped along the deserted main street and out of town.

Neither man spoke as they rode, eager to put as much distance as they could between them and the posse that would surely follow.

Elliott was still surprised at what he had done by helping a convicted killer escape. It had been an act of desperation, but it all seemed so stupid now as he rode and wondered what he was hoping to achieve. It wasn't as though Makin had confessed to raping Eleanor. He might not have even been in the vicinity at the time, and supposing it was him, how was that going to help. Makin was hardly likely to offer to cooperate because he couldn't without bringing about a new date for his hanging. Stanton realized that the thought of the man who might be able to help him being dead in four or five hours had made him panic into hasty action.

Elliott's horse was the faster of the two and he was always a couple of lengths ahead. By the time they stopped close to the base of a small group of rocks both horses were badly in need of a rest. Elliott guessed that they must have been riding for over an hour and so far there was no sign of a posse. With luck no one would enter the office and discover their disappearance for quite some time. One thing was certain, Eli wouldn't manage to escape from the chair, not after the way that Makin had tied the strips of blanket.

Makin was breathing almost as heavily as his horse after the efforts of the hard ride. After he had taken a long swig from the water canteen he took a while before he recovered from a bout of coughing.

'Why did you rescue me, Hogan? It's not as though I owe you anything. You were free to go and now you're in big trouble. What gives?'

Elliott had been expecting the question and decided that he might as well confront Makin right here and now.

'It's a long story but a simple one. After listening to all your bragging about how you forced yourself on women I believe that you could be the man who raped the woman I was going to marry.'

Makin gave his usual sly snigger. 'What, you mean your woman got herself poked and you think it was me? Well, as I said there have been so many I'm not sure that I could really remember. To be honest, once they're on their backs with their legs open, there's not a lot of difference, unless they have something special about them that sort of sticks in your mind. I once had a woman who had the biggest pair of milkers you've ever seen, even bigger than Angie's who works at the Jerome Palace. Now I remember her.'

Elliott was getting angry at the flippant way Makin was talking, but he had to stay focused and continued, 'It happened near Fort Isaac about three months ago. She was fair haired and pretty and I was with her at the time.'

'Then you should have protected her, Hogan. So now you're feeling guilty because you let someone take her and he made you watch. That's it I reckon.'

'It wasn't like that at all. I just want you to tell me if it was you,' said Elliott as he struggled to control his anger at the crude remarks from the animal that he had set free. Elliott moved his hand close to his gun even though Makin was still unarmed.

'It might have been me,' Makin remarked casually. 'I've had a few army women. They're usually hungry for it with their men folk being away and they don't usually need forcing into it.'

Makin was clearly enjoying teasing Elliott, showing not the slightest bit of sympathy or any gratitude for helping him escape the hanging.

'Just give me a straight answer, yes or no,' shouted Elliott as he drew his gun.

'Ain't any good you waving that thing at me, you won't shoot an unarmed man. You're not the type, I can tell. Anyway, what's the point? If I tell you it wasn't me, you'll still wonder if I am telling you the truth. So I'll make it easier for you. Yes, it was me. I remember that sweet young thing with the golden hair. A classy lady as I recall and she did fight back more than most, but I don't remember seeing you there.'

Elliott tensed his trigger finger, wanting to shoot the pathetic excuse for a human being who was smiling at him.

'Get on your horse,' Elliott ordered. 'I'm taking you back to Fort Isaac where I was a Lieutenant. I expect you'll be handed back to the sheriff for the hanging that you deserve after they have questioned you.'

'You can kiss my ass,' replied Makin. 'I'm not riding anywhere with you. Why should I? If you had any sense you'd get well away from here. You seem to have forgotten that you helped me escape and the town won't take too kindly for what you did to that little runt, Eli.'

'I left a message with Eli to give to the sheriff. He'll understand why I did it once I explain to him, and Eli wasn't harmed too much, but I don't intend to get caught by the posse.'

Makin laughed out loud. 'I would say having a knife in the belly was harmful enough and the sort of thing that would get a man hung.'

'What are you talking about?' Elliott asked and then he remembered that Makin had gone back into the office to collect his baccy.

'That little runt got what he deserved, but if you take me back then I'll tell the sheriff that it was you that did it and Jerome will have a double hanging. I've seen enough dead men to know that Eli was good and dead when I last saw him.'

'You're lying. I didn't see any knife in the office,' said Elliott.

Makin reached inside his shirt and removed a piece of blanket which he unwrapped to reveal a small knife.

'This little beauty is mine and was in the drawer of the sheriff's desk. Now I'm riding out of here and if you have any sense you'll do the same.'

Elliott followed slowly behind Makin as he walked towards his horse. He was thinking that it would help if he waited until Makin was mounted, and Elliott's action seemed to puzzle Makin who eyed him suspiciously as he swung himself in to the saddle. Elliott reacted with speed and was mounted himself just seconds later, and pointed his pistol at Makin's back.

'Now ride out towards the fort or I'll shoot you — and that's a promise,' Elliott threatened.

Makin turned around and sniggered once more. 'I'm betting that you have never shot a man in your life and you ain't got the guts to do it now. I'll see you around, soldier boy.'

Makin's mount was no more than a couple of horse-lengths away when the bullet struck him in the shoulder causing him to crash to the ground. By the time he had staggered to his feet and tried to reach the wounded shoulder, Elliott had dismounted and was standing nearby, his pistol trained on Makin.

'You stupid bastard, I didn't rape your woman. I was just playing with you. I figured you wrong but I'm still not going to any fort with you, so you had better finish me off or leave me unless you plan to lift me on to that horse, because I ain't moving.'

Elliott had only shot Makin to stop him from escaping, but he wasn't certain if Makin was any use to him. Perhaps Makin was telling the truth when he had said that he hadn't raped Eleanor. Even if he had, Makin wasn't going to do him any favours, especially now that he'd just shot him. The more he thought about it the more he realized that he'd got himself into more trouble for no good reason. He would leave Makin here and get clear away so he could decide what his next move would be. Elliott's decision would have been made for him anyway as he spotted the posse who were no more than a couple of hundred yards away.

Makin watched Elliott mount his horse. 'Why don't you stay and tell your little story to the sheriff, soldier,' he sniggered. 'I'll put in a good word for you.'

'Shut your filthy mouth, Makin. If you really did attack my sweet girl then I hope they hang you very slowly.' Elliott mounted and rode away, hoping that Makin had lied about killing Eli and that the posse would settle for Makin's recapture and let him go. He was well clear when he heard shots being fired and he turned to look. The posse had stopped near where he had left Makin and he was too far away for the shots to be aimed at him. The horse was going as fast as it could possibly go but he instinctively used his heels once more in the hope of some extra speed.

'Shall we go after him, Sheriff?' asked one of the men who had fired one of the shots at Makin.

'No, let him go. I don't know what that feller was up to with Makin, but it don't matter none now. Makin's dead and the town won't be having a hanging after all.'

Eli had been trailing behind the posse and he edged his mount forward and smiled down at the body of the man who had punched him when he was strapped to the chair in the sheriff's office.

'Do you think that feller might have known Makin from prison, Sheriff?' Eli asked. 'And I wonder what he meant about getting Makin to clear his name.'

The sheriff shrugged his shoulders. 'Who knows, Eli. Makin was locked up for nearly two years until they let him out a month ago. You think he would have learned a lesson after all that time, but it didn't stop him sniffing after women that didn't belong to him. I didn't get the impression that they knew each other and that feller didn't seem the type to keep company with someone like Makin.'

Sheriff Tatum turned over Makin's body and saw the shoulder wound that couldn't have been caused by one of the posse. 'I'll tell you one thing, that feller was no friend of Makin,' said the sheriff as he watched Elliott disappear from view.

12

It was well past the time when Nell Stanton would normally have retired to bed, but she knew that sleep would not come easy and was enjoying the late evening air as she sat on the porch. Recent events had turned her world upside down and she had to be close to exhaustion before she could drop off to sleep. Her faith had been tested so much in recent months, but she believed that whatever tragedy came her way, it was for a purpose. God wasn't cruel. He was difficult to understand at times but he wasn't cruel. Life was about good and bad. Good and bad people and good and bad times.

A terrible injustice had been brought upon her dear son, but he was alive and he would come through all of this. She had tried to persuade her husband to have the same belief, but his faith wasn't as strong and he was hurt by some of the comments he heard when he went to town. Not from the people who had known Elliott but from some of the newcomers. He should have ignored them but he was a proud man and couldn't walk away from trouble. Then three weeks ago when he was in town a man had shouted from across the street, 'Lock up your daughters, folks. Like father like son.' Will had snapped and would have killed the man if the sheriff hadn't pulled him off. But he gave the man a really bad beating and it upset him greatly. That night he had complained of pains in his chest. The following morning he couldn't speak and had lost all feeling down his right side.

★ ★ ★

The light was fading by the time Elliot reached the signpost that showed that he was two miles from Traycora and the point where he had to leave the trail. It was a clear night but still dark enough to force him to slow down with just a mile to go before he would reach home. The journey from Jerome had been uneventful and he had only stopped for a couple of hours' sleep the previous night, eager to see his sick pa and his ma. When he reached the small homestead where he'd been born he felt good despite the reason that brought him here. There were so many happy memories here that it would have been hard not to have felt that way. If his ma had not had such problems giving birth to him then there would have been more children, but his had been a happy childhood and there had been lots of friends from the neighbouring farms. He knew that his pa was disappointed when he'd told him of his plans to enlist. How different things would have been now if he had heeded his pa's wish and stayed home. Will Stanton had told him the importance of having roots and being near folks that you could trust. He had warned him to be on his guard because he would meet up with men that were thieves and even murderers. Some of them would sell their own grandmother for a dollar and that was a fact.

Nell jumped nervously when she heard the porch floorboards creak.

'Don't be frightened, Mrs Stanton. It's me, Tommy.'

'Young Tommy, you startled me. Is there something wrong?' Nell asked.

'No, ma'am, I just came to tell you that there's someone here who you will want to see, even though its so late.'

Nell Stanton didn't want to see any callers, no matter how well-meaning they might be, not tonight. She was about to tell Tommy Jackson, who worked for her, to send them away when the figure appeared from the darkness behind Tommy.

'It's me, ma, its Elliott,'

As the shaggy-haired man stepped on to the porch she could see that he looked nothing like her Elliott, but there was no mistaking the voice.

Tommy choked up when he saw them embrace and he retreated quietly from the porch and headed back to his bunkhouse.

'Your pa's gone, son. I only buried him this afternoon,' Nell blurted out, eager to relay the sad news to her son. 'I've done so much praying lately and at least one of my prayers has been answered, now that you are here.'

'Ma, I know all about pa. I got a message that he was sick and that's why I came home; Tommy told me about him dying.'

Stanton led his ma inside the house and in the light he could see how much she had changed. She had aged so much in such a short time and he knew that it wasn't all down to the upset of his pa. He knew her worrying about him had also contributed to the change, and it made him feel bad as well as angry, but he was determined that he wouldn't let her see his own upset. He would need to be strong and put aside his own grieving for the short time that he would be there. Folks say that sons are usually closer to their mother but it had never been the case with him. He had loved them both but he had worshipped his pa. His pa had been everything that a son would ever want him to be. He had been as strong as an ox, wise in so many ways, patient with him when he was trying to teach him new things. Most of Elliott's strengths and skills had come from his pa, who had also taught him to be a man more than his life in army had. Even though Will Stanton was approaching old age he had still seemed indestructible to his son. He had never known him have a day's illness in his life. He had seen him shrug off serious injuries resulting from accidents around the farm and now he was gone. Whatever the cause, Stanton believed that his pa would be alive and his ma would not be looking old before her time if it wasn't for what had happened to him. As he cradled his sobbing ma, Elliott silently repeated the vow to make someone pay and pay dearly one day.

He had let her talk, knowing that it would help. Some of the stories he had heard many times, but others were new. Perhaps it was because deep down she sensed that she might never see him again, and she was anxious to fill in any missing gaps about their family background. He heard tales of a place called Shropshire in England where pa's family had been farmers and of the big house were she had been a kind of servant before her own pa and ma had brought the family to the big country. It was painful when she recounted how pa used to tell all his friends about his boy, the US Cavalry Officer.

'He was so proud of you, son, right up to the day he left us. I've got to tell you this, Elliott, even though it hurts me so. The last words that he spoke were . . . ' Nell was unable to continue because of her sobbing. She tried several times, repeating the same word between sobs before she finally said, 'When you see that boy of ours, tell him that I loved him from the time he gave his first cry and I still love him. He had only whispered a 'thank you' and a faint smile during the last few days before he died, but he managed that message for you, son. He so much wanted to have a son, and the day that you were born I swear that there couldn't have been a happier man in the whole world than your pa.'

It was the first time that Nell had ever seen a grown man cry, but she wasn't surprised that Elliott had. Her boy had lost more than a father; he had lost the man who she knew had been his inspiration. She wondered how he would cope with the loss of his pa after everything else that had happened to him and hoped that the memory of his pa would give him the strength that he would need.

Later that night Elliott told his ma that he had killed a man in self-defence, thinking it best that she heard it from him. He explained his time with the Ashleys, but not about his illness or any of details that might stress her. Nell explained about Everson's visit and how he was anxious to talk to him about new evidence, but Everson hadn't mentioned anything about a killing. Ma thought that Everson was such a nice man, taking the trouble to come and see them. Elliott just wasn't sure about Everson any more and would be reluctant to trust him.

It was barely light when Elliott said his heart-wrenching goodbye to his ma, and she asked him once again to go as far away as possible to avoid being captured and for him not to worry about her. Tommy Jackson was a good man and he would look after the place. She would sooner she never saw him again than have Elliott face a life of being hunted and perhaps caught and executed for killing the man in self-defence.

'You can't rely upon justice, son, you should know that by now. You must think very carefully before following Lieutenant Everson's advice.'

'I don't just want justice for me, ma. I want it for Eleanor, pa and for you as well. But don't worry, I'll be careful whatever I decide to do.'

★   ★   ★

He was glad to see Tommy Jackson was already up as he walked by the tiny cabin that his pa had built for the hired help to live in, and he was able to tell Tommy that he hoped to be back soon, but not to mention this to his ma. He gave a final wave to the sad figure on the porch and headed for his pa's resting place. Tommy had told him that there were still some soldiers in town but he wasn't sure if they were looking for him.

He had only been to the graveyard once and that was to attend his Uncle Ben's funeral just before he left for West Point. He had no trouble locating his pa's grave with the mass of flowers around it. The message that had been carved in the wooden cross was simple:

'With Love, devoted wife, Nell and son, Elliott'.

He kneeled down beside the grave and raked away a deep hole beneath the cross. He then reached inside his shirt for the sheepskin pouch that contained the medal that had belonged to Grandpa Stanton, who had died in some long-forgotten war. He placed the pouch in the hole and covered it with soil and then firmed it down with his fist.

'I'll be back for it, Pa, and that's a promise,' was all he said before mounting his pa's black horse and riding off on his return journey to see the Ashleys and explain why he had gone missing.

13

He had covered the first few miles of the journey that would take him back to the Ashleys when he spotted the man ahead who was crouched down attending to his horse. It was probably his imagination, but he had a feeling someone had been following him since he had left his pa's graveside and seeing the man gave him a strange sort of comfort.

The man let the horse's leg return to the standing position and stood up. 'Howdy! My horse picked up a stone back there.'

Elliott returned the man's greeting. He seemed friendly enough so he offered to help him.

'Thanks, but I think I've just about done it. Where're you heading for?'

'I'm going to Fort Isaac to enlist in the army,' lied Elliott. It didn't seem likely that this man would have any interest in him, but best to be on the safe side. As a precaution he introduced himself once again as Jed Hogan.

'They call me John L. Travan amongst other things. I'm heading for Jerome to see my sister who has just been made a widow so I'm going to make sure that she's doing all right. Maybe we could ride together, if you don't mind the company.'

Elliott didn't see any harm with the suggestion, but there was something familiar about Travan and he was certain that he'd seen him before.

* * *

They rode hard for most of the day and made good progress even though Travan did slow them down a bit, partly because his sorrel couldn't match the speed of Elliott's fine mount — plus he had the handicap of a large basket that was strapped to his saddle.

They were less than twenty miles

from Jerome when the fading light caused them to make camp for the night. Travan had hardly said a word for most of the journey and when Elliott offered to share his food with him, Travan had rejected the offer in an aggressive manner. Elliott had been lost in his own thoughts for most of the journey so he hadn't minded the silence, but he was taken aback by Travan's change of mood. They had eaten their food separately and in silence and Elliott was preparing to bed down for the night by the camp fire when Travan, who had been sitting some distance away, came over carrying the basket. Elliott could smell the whiskey that Travan had been swigging from a large bottle ever since they had stopped. Elliott was curious to know what was in the basket, which had been placed close to him.

'I'm going to show you something that not many men get to see, Stanton, but you had better be very quiet and very still.'

Travan's speech had been slurred but there was no mistaking that he had called him Stanton. Travan opened the lid of the basket and then stepped back to the other side of the fire. Elliott had guessed the contents just a moment before the head of the snake appeared.

'Let me introduce you to my friend Sabre. He's an Arizona Coral and he's a killer. If you move and he doesn't like you then you'll be a dead man, Stanton. Yes I did say Stanton. You're Lieutenant Elliott Stanton, rapist and the murderer of my brother, Sergeant Nolan, and tomorrow, I'm taking you back to Fort Isaac to collect myself a small mountain of money as my reward.'

Stanton's eyes were fixed on the snake when he heard the familiar sound of a weapon being drawn from its holster. He had already removed his own gun belt when he had prepared to bed down for the night, not that it would have been much use to him at the moment. Travan removed any temptation Elliott might have had when he picked up the gun belt and flung it some distance away. Travan was unsteady on his feet as he moved, so that he was now standing behind the basket and Elliott could see that he was filled with anger. Elliott didn't know how he had been identified but still hoped to talk his way out of trouble.

'You must be mistaking me for someone else, John. I've already told you that I'm going to Fort Isaac, so why would I be doing that if I was wanted by the army. I've never known anyone by the name of Nolan and I certainly didn't kill your brother.'

'Yeah, that's got me puzzled, unless you were planning on giving yourself up, Stanton. But it don't matter none now.'

It seemed strange hearing his real name being used again and he was baffled by the accusation about Sergeant Nolan. As Elliott studied the man's face in the light of the fire, he realized why he had thought he had met him before. He was much smaller built than Sergeant Nolan, but there was certainly a likeness about their faces and little doubt that they were brothers.

Elliott asked Travan what made him so sure that he was a man by the name of Stanton.

'I'm damned sure that you're Elliott Stanton. I've been holed up watching your folk's place for best part of two weeks. When you didn't show up for the funeral yesterday I was planning on moving on, but when I saw you hugging your old ma this morning I was a happy man. By the way that was a nice gesture, you visiting your pa's grave.'

Elliott didn't see the point of trying to bluff his way any more. 'I am Elliott Stanton but I'm innocent. If I wasn't then I would have crossed the border into Mexico by now. Sergeant Nolan let me escape and he was alive when I rode out of the fort.'

'Sure he was,' Travan sniggered. 'Why would he just let you go free? I went to the fort to see my brother and they told me that you had knifed him and then escaped. My brother was a professional soldier and you're a liar as well as a murderer. I would have hunted you down for free, but someone at the fort wants your hide real bad and he's prepared to pay me a lot more than the official reward.'

'Did Colonel Danvers hire you?' Stanton asked. The colonel came from a rich family and financing a large reward wouldn't be a problem for him, and who could blame him.

'No, I ain't working for Danvers, but I don't intend to tell you who it is that probably wishes you dead just as much as me and Danvers. I met him when I was at the fort and he offered a stack of money to catch you. As I've already said I would have done it for nothing.'

'If your brother really is dead then his killer is back at Fort Isaac now because I didn't kill him. I swear I didn't,' pleaded Elliott.

'I ain't interested in what you've got to say. Now shut your mouth before you upset Sabre. By the way, in case you're wondering, Sabre would never harm me. Snake breeding used to be a hobby of mine when I was settled in my own place and I weaned Sabre as if I was his own ma. Some folks will tell you that a bite from an Arizona Coral will not kill you and that a snake will not harm you unless you upset it. Well that's hogwash and if you don't believe me then I'll be taking you back to Fort Isaac all cold and stiff. I ain't saying that Sabre will kill you quickly but he's twice the average size and delivers a mighty load of venom. You might even go mad before you die because the poison sometimes attacks the brain but you'll die. Now, I'm going to bed down over there and finish off my whiskey. I don't think that I need tie you up because you'll still be there in the morning, whether you're dead or alive depending upon how still you keep.'

Elliott could hear Travan gulping from the whiskey bottle, and it wasn't long before he heard what must have been the empty bottle being tossed away.

Travan's speech was even more slurred as he tried to tell Elliott a story about 'his friend Sabre'. There were some gaps in the story and other parts of it were repeated, but it seemed that Travan had suspected that his wife had been unfaithful to him with one of his friends. Then he had come home one day and found them both dead in bed. Travan had told folks that he felt so guilty about Sabre getting out of his basket. Travan must have laughed himself to sleep after he had finished telling the tale and was soon snoring.

Just as the fire was about to finally flicker and die the snake retreated back into the basket and Elliott was preparing to slam the lid down when the head reappeared, and Elliott was about to spend the most nerve-racking night of his life.

It had been worse when the fire had gone out. Sometimes he could still see the head of his guardian, but not when the moon was hidden by the clouds. The intense concentration of trying to keep still must have tired him so much that he lost the battle to stay awake.

* * *

It was light when he woke up and he moved before he remembered the bizarre events of the previous night, and his eyes focused on the basket. Having moved once without being punished for it, he turned his head very slowly in the direction of where Travan had bedded down. His captor's face was a strange pallor and his eyes where staring up at the sky.

'Travan,' Elliott called out. But there was no response. By the time that Elliott had called out three more times, each call louder than the previous one, there was still no response. Elliott decided that Travan either slept with his eyes open or he was dead. Elliott didn't know anything about the sleeping habits of snakes, but he was ready to gamble that Sabre was either at the bottom of the basket or out of striking range. He slowly moved towards the basket and flipped the lid closed. He wasn't about to confirm whether the snake was inside or not and settled for turning the basket upside-down to prevent the snake from forcing its way out.

A closer look at Travan revealed a large lump on the side of his neck and it had an ugly red mark at its centre. There was no doubt that he was dead and mostly likely the victim of Sabre or perhaps another snake who had been attracted to the spot by Sabre. Elliott figured that Sabre had probably slid over next to Travan during the night and perhaps Travan had lashed out at it during his drunken sleep or rolled over on to it.

★ ★ ★

Elliott stripped the saddle from Travan's horse and let it run loose. An inspection of Travan's belongings had revealed a large sum of money and some documents that confirmed his story that he was Nolan's brother. There was also a crumpled poster that was a good likeness of how Elliott had once looked and it confirmed that he was wanted for the murder. The ground nearby was reasonably soft and Elliott managed to dig out a shallow grave which he dragged Travan's body into. Before he left the campsite he carefully picked up the basket and flung it as far as he could away from the trail, unsure if it was still occupied but not wanting a passer-by to investigate its contents.

14

Elliott had continued his journey to the Ashley place but decided to stay the night in the soddy that he had repaired on the day that the Coogans had jumped him. The news that Sergeant Nolan was dead had changed everything. It seemed very likely that whoever had killed Nolan was involved in the rape, perhaps the same man who had hired Travan. Elliott hoped that if he gave himself up, knowing that he was wanted for Nolan's murder, then it might help his case. Colonel Danvers would want the real rapist to be caught and he was bound to have second thoughts about Elliott's guilt if he had surrendered knowing that he would face execution. Elliott's spirits were higher than at any point since he had escaped from Fort Isaac. He recalled his talk with Hawky about him being wanted for murder when Elliott had wrongly assumed that he was referring to Bollinger's murder and not Nolan's. If he had known about Nolan he wouldn't have made the visit to Jerome which nearly ended in disaster. The most important thing now was for him to get to the fort and surrender before he was captured. He would do it tomorrow, but not before he had made a visit to the Ashleys.

★　★　★

It was early morning when Elliott approached the farmhouse where he had nearly died, and he began to wonder if he was doing the right thing returning. Perhaps he should have left things as they were, but he felt that he owed it to them to explain the reason for his absence.

Tom Ashley was on the porch and Elliott's concerns about what sort of reception he would get were soon answered by a scowl on Tom's face that he hadn't seen before.

'Was there something you wanted here, boy?' Tom asked. 'Did you leave something behind when you left without a word? I don't mind telling you how disappointed I was and it upset Emma as well.'

Elliott had expected them to be a little cool towards him, but not hostile. Any hopes that Emma might not feel bad towards him were also dashed when she came out, gave him a cold glance before going back inside the house. He felt hurt being rejected by folks that he liked so much, knowing that he hadn't done anything wrong, but he had other things more worrying to think about.

'I didn't mean to upset you folks and that's why I've come back to explain. I'll always be grateful to you and Emma, but I can see that I've hurt you both and I'm sorry but I won't be bothering you again. Goodbye Tom.' Elliott turned his mount and prepared to ride off.

'Now hold on there, son,' Tom called after him. 'I guess a man deserves a chance to explain, but whatever you've got to tell us, it had better be the truth.'

Elliott dismounted and climbed the two steps to the porch, relieved that he would be able to correct the misunderstanding. 'Then perhaps I had better start with Jonty Coogan's visit here a few weeks ago while you were away in town.' Elliott couldn't see how it would do any harm to mention the incident now. It was likely that the Coogans had left the district and there would be no risk of Tom tackling Jonty for what he had tried to do to Emma.

'Coogan was here!' Tom questioned. 'Emma never mentioned anything about Coogan being here.'

'Its true, Pa,' said Emma as she reappeared on the porch. 'Jonty came here pestering me and Jed chased him off the place.'

Elliott told them about the brothers attacking him and then him being rescued by an old friend who had come to tell him about his pa being sick. Tom and Emma said how sorry they were for being so distant with him and Emma cried when he explained about his pa dying. He told them that he had some things to sort out, but gave no details of what it was about. He told Tom that he would be happy to help out for the rest of the day but he would be leaving before dark. Tom as always was grateful for any help he could get and asked Elliott to replace some rotten wood on the porch and help him clean out the big barn. He caught Emma looking at him a few times and he knew that she was upset about him leaving again.

During supper, both Tom and Emma asked him to stay and he was tempted to tell them the full story, but he just told them that what he had to do was personal and they backed off. He was pleased to have been able to see them again and explain things about his departure but it was hard when he said goodbye and headed for the barn which he used as his sleeping quarters and got ready to leave for Fort Isaac.

He had hung up the uniform that he brought back from his home and it didn't look too creased. The pinned-back hair looked reasonably presentable and he had trimmed the shaggy beard. He now looked more like Lieutenant Elliott Stanton of the US Army than Jed Hogan the drifter, and as he placed the hat on to his head he felt like a soldier again. The pride had returned and he knew that he was doing the right thing. Not just for his ma's sake and the memory of his pa, but for himself.

He was leading his saddled mount away from the barn when he saw the approaching figure and he froze for a moment before Emma came forward. She made as though to challenge him and then gave a little gasp as she raised her hand to cover her mouth.

'I'd like to explain to you but I can't, not now,' he said, seeing how shocked his new appearance had been for her.

'I knew that there was something about you but I just didn't know what,'

Emma shouted. 'You're up to no good and I hate you for coming back telling us all those lies.'

'Emma, I promise you that I've done nothing to be ashamed of. But I am in trouble and I'm going to try and clear my name. I am going to Fort Isaac and do something that I should have done before now. The story about my father is true and I haven't told you or Tom any lies other than who I really am.'

'You must be a deserter, but why did you come back into our lives and get us to . . . ' She didn't finish off what she really wanted to say as the tears appeared in her eyes.

'I can't explain it to you now. I can only ask you to trust me. I came back because I wanted to see you again. I could easily have stayed away but that's not what I wanted.'

Emma was sobbing as she spoke and pleaded with him to stay. 'You know how much you mean to us both and that you can trust us. If you're in trouble then you'll be safe here working with pa.'

He wanted to tell her that he wished that he could stay with her forever. That he loved her, perhaps even more than he had Eleanor, something that he had never thought possible. He knew that by not revealing his feelings for her she would feel rejected, because he felt certain that she loved him.

When she sobbed and begged him to stay he knew that he couldn't leave her like this because it would destroy her. He hugged her to him and then lifted her head and smothered her cheeks with light kisses before their lips met.

As they separated from the kiss, Emma was calm and assured in a way that she had never experienced before. 'Why didn't you kiss me like that weeks ago?' she asked. Her face was flushed and smiling.

'You will never know just how much I wanted to, but I couldn't,' he replied smiling back at her.

Emma was once again anxious.

'You're not married, Jed?' she asked and then she remembered what he had said and then added, 'But Jed's not your real name is it?'

'The answer is no to both those questions. My real name is Elliott Stanton. Lieutenant Elliott Stanton.' Now it was his turn to be anxious as he wondered if she had heard the name before, perhaps from her pa. If she had then there would be no point in hiding the story from her.

'Elliott, Elliott,' she mused over it for a while and then teased him. 'I like Jed better. No, Elliott is better, but it'll take me a while to get used to it.'

'Let's go into the barn,' said Elliott and he took hold of her hand. 'There are some things that I need to explain and it looks as though I won't be leaving until tomorrow now.'

Once inside the barn he lit the oil lamp and could see how flushed Emma was with the excitement of what had happened. She was truly beautiful and the scar was fainter than when he first saw it now that her face had been tanned by the recent sunshine. The brightness and love in those blue eyes would have won the attention over the most hideous of disfigurements, let alone a faded line of scar tissue.

They sat on a bale of hay and he kissed her again, briefly and lightly before he broke away.

'I said I wasn't married and I'm not, but I am sort of in the same position really.'

She gave him a puzzled look and was about to speak when he gently placed a finger across her lips.

'It's just that I am not free to get involved with you until I have settled a very important matter at the fort, but its risky and if things go wrong, you may never see me again.'

'But I don't understand. It all sounds so mysterious and frightening. Is there someone waiting for you at the fort, a woman?'

Elliott smiled. 'No, there's no other woman. It's just that I have been wrongly accused of something very serious and I have got to go back and clear my name.'

'Then you will be back here tomorrow night and we can tell pa how we feel about each other. He will be so thrilled for us. I know he likes you so much, just like a son.'

The smile had gone from his face as he explained. 'It may not be that simple, Emma. I can't tell you any more except to say that I want you to know that I am innocent. I want you to remember that. I wanted to ride off tonight and not get too involved, in fairness to you.'

'But I want to be involved. Why won't you let me try and help?' she pleaded.

'There's nothing you can do, Emma, and you're going to have to trust me. We can talk a little more tomorrow, but now you had better get back to your pa and tell him that I'll be leaving early in the morning instead of tonight. Perhaps it's best if we keep our feelings a secret for now. Just remember that I love you, Emma.'

They kissed in the same way that sweethearts do when the man is going off to war, knowing that they might never see each other ever again.

Elliott didn't sleep much that night as he realized that tomorrow he would be risking not just his freedom, but for the second time in his life he might lose a woman that he loved.

15

Hawky hadn't slept much either the night before Elliott had planned to give himself up. He had been reliving the meeting that he had had with Lieutenant Everson. The lieutenant had seemed genuinely elated when he told him that he could help Stanton, and that he had discovered that when Stanton was first arrested on the day of the rape none of the buttons were missing from his uniform. Everson didn't reveal how he had come by this information, but did say that had this been known at the trial then Stanton would never have been found guilty. According to Everson he had also heard that the Governor was going to pardon a number of men, and if Stanton gave himself up then Everson could present a strong case for his release now that he had new evidence. When Hawky had mentioned that

Stanton was also wanted for murder, the lieutenant was confident that a strong case could be made due to mitigating circumstances.

When Hawky set off early the next morning for the ride to the Ashley place he still had doubts about the whole thing, but figured that he didn't have any choice but to tell Lieutenant Stanton and let him decide for himself. He didn't fully understand everything that Everson had told him and he didn't completely trust the man. By the time that Hawky pulled up his pure black stallion outside the Ashley place, he was hoping that the lieutenant wasn't there. At least his conscience would be clear after having tried to locate him, but, with luck, he might still be with his folks. There was also the chance that the lieutenant had put aside his pride and was a long, long way from here. Hawky was already feeling jumpy and the woman's screams didn't help matters. He had never seen anyone appear so frightened as she fled indoors, and he was relieved when Lieutenant Stanton appeared from the same door that the woman had hid behind.

Elliott smiled and then called out, 'Emma, this is Hawky, the man who saved me from the Coogans and much more.' Emma reappeared and stood behind Elliott and then a shy smile appeared as she spoke to Hawky. 'I'm sorry, it's just that we don't get many, hmm, strangers here and you gave me a fright.'

Tom Ashley had joined them on the porch and he looked beyond Hawky. 'It looks like we got some other company this morning, honey.' Hawky turned and saw the group of soldiers headed by a smirking Everson. If he hadn't been so preoccupied with his reservations about the trip he would have realized that he was being followed.

'I'm sorry, Lieutenant. I've been tricked, I — '

Hawky's words were cut off by Everson who had ridden up behind him. 'You have done well, Hawky. Colonel Danvers will be pleased with you for hunting down this man.'

The two soldiers who had already dismounted moved forward swiftly and dragged Elliott off the porch and threw him to the ground. Two more soldiers appeared and one of them was carrying a rope, which they used to bind Elliott's hands and legs. He twisted his head to try and see the distraught Emma, wanting to have a final look, hoping that she would see the sorrow in his face.

Emma was hysterical as she screamed out, 'He's innocent. He was going to give himself up today. Why are you treating him like that?'

'Maybe because he's a rapist and murdered a fellow soldier,' Everson replied.

Elliott was wishing that he had told her about Eleanor and that he hadn't murdered anyone. He finally managed to wriggle his body around and saw the doubt in her face and the look of disgust that Tom Ashley was giving him.

Emma's doubts had soon gone, or she didn't care as she shouted at her pa, 'But he's innocent, pa. Do something, help him.'

Tom Ashley put a comforting arm around her shoulders. 'If he's innocent then he's got nothing to fear, honey. Come on, let's go inside.'

'That's good advice, sir. I'm afraid that this man tells a convincing story. I almost believed him myself once. But innocent men don't murder their own comrades in arms. This man is a disgrace to the uniform of the US Cavalry, but not for much longer. Good day to you folks.'

Elliott had been bundled onto a horse and the party rode away as a sobbing Emma was led inside.

During the journey back to Fort Isaac, Elliott was subjected to a continuous string of abuse and threats connected with him having killed Sergeant Nolan when he made his escape.

The short distance from the entrance to Fort Isaac and the jailhouse was lined with soldiers. There were loud cheers as the men tossed their hats in the air and some let out whoops of joy. It was yet another humiliating experience for him, but for the man standing alone on the porch of the main HQ building it was a moment of relief. The man was Colonel Danvers, who had begun to despair that they would ever bring Stanton to justice. Sergeant Nolan had been a fine soldier, perhaps the best that Danvers had ever had under his command and he was sorry that he was dead. But from the moment he had heard the news that the Sergeant had been murdered he realized that Stanton was no longer going to jail, he was going to die. Elliott was dragged from his horse and thrown into the same cell that he had occupied before. He was punched, kicked and spat at by his handlers before he collapsed onto the hard bed. At least being dazed prevented the mental pain of thinking about the desperate position he was now in. There would be plenty of time for agonizing about how Emma would be coping; sweet, vulnerable Emma who had seen her life turned upside-down in such a short time.

He didn't hear the rattle of the keys, nor was he aware that two men had entered his cell and one of them dragged him to his feet.

'Officer present,' someone roared in his ear. Through squinted eyes, he saw the face of Captain Pearmain.

'Sergeant Crowe! Who did this to the prisoner?' Pearmain asked as he noticed the bloodied face of Elliott.

'The prisoner became violent when he was being put into the cell, sir, and he fell and injured himself.'

Sergeant Crowe was Sergeant Nolan's replacement and the man mostly responsible for the present state of Elliott's face.

'I will not tolerate any mistreatment of prisoners. Is that clear?' Pearmain shouted at the Sergeant. The order was accompanied by a smile and a wink.

'Yes sir,' Crowe replied with a smile.

'Help the prisoner back onto the bed before he collapses and then leave us alone, Sergeant,' Pearmain ordered as he took out a piece of folded paper from the inside of his tunic.

Sergeant Crowe gave Pearmain a quizzical look. 'Are you sure that's wise, sir, what with him being a slippery customer from what I've heard.'

Pearmain looked down at the pathetic figure of Stanton who was struggling to focus his eyes. 'I think I can manage thank you, Sergeant.'

Once Sergeant Crowe had left the cell Pearmain unfolded the paper and proceeded to read.

'Elliott James Stanton, you will be charged with, and tried for, the murder of Sergeant Edward Nolan during your escape from the garrison prison at Fort Isaac on 9 January 1887. Should you be found not guilty I expect the court will review your sentence for the rape of

Miss Eleanor Danvers in light of your escape.'

Pearmain folded the paper and replaced it inside his tunic and then added as an afterthought, 'The trial will be held here at Fort Isaac one week from today. Is there anything you wish to say at this stage?'

'Not guilty,' was all that Elliott said in what was no more than a whisper.

'As you wish. I must inform you that in view of your escape you will not be allowed any visitors, nor will you be allowed to leave the cell to take any form of exercise. I don't know what happened to you along the way, Stanton, but at least all this will soon be over for all of us, especially my uncle. I don't expect that I will see you again so try and remember that you were an officer and go out with some dignity. Did you hear any of what I have said?'

Elliott managed to croak out the briefest acknowledgement and raised his hand. He could just about make out the features of Pearmain. The only problem was that he could see more than one figure as a result of his concussion.

Pearmain was intent on delivering his own personal message before he left and had not the slightest sympathy for the pathetic figure that lay in front of him. 'For the record, Stanton, I never liked you. I am sure that you never intended for my cousin to die the way that she did, but you caused her death and you killed an innocent man rather than take your punishment. Your actions are proof that I was right when I told my cousin that she shouldn't have got involved with someone who was outside her social class. If she had listened to me then she would have been alive today.'

There was no response and Pearmain was clearly amused at Stanton's discomfort and was eager to go and report the prisoner's condition to his uncle.

'Sergeant Crowe, I'm ready to leave now.'

Sergeant Crowe entered the cell and

bent down to roar in Elliott's ear. 'Officer leaving, prisoner will stand.'

Pearmain waved a hand at Crowe. 'I think we can dispense with that Sergeant Crowe, unless you want to hold him up yourself. I'm not sure if the poor wretch will still be alive come the trial. Perhaps you ought to get one of the medics to look at him, but don't bother Dr Simmons. I expect he's got more deserving cases to busy himself with.'

'Yes, sir,' roared Crowe.

Pearmain turned back and spoke though the cell bars.

'I forgot to mention that you will of course be allowed some form of legal representation. The only problem is that there are not likely to be many volunteers wishing to associate themselves with you. Everson has already asked not to be appointed, but someone will be found and then they will come and speak with you.'

16

It was almost light when Elliott opened his eyes. He felt a searing pain each time he drew breath and wondered how many ribs had been broken this time. The throb from his nose indicated another breakage and an exploratory feel with his tongue inside his bloodied mouth revealed some loose teeth. It was difficult to separate what he might have been dreaming from fact. Did Pearmain really visit him? Did he mention a trial and those other things? At least he could see perfectly well. He managed a rueful smile when he realized that it didn't really matter any more. He had lost any thoughts of miracles or vengeance. He was a broken man who had come to accept that he had been dealt a cruel hand in life. His thoughts turned to religion and to a God that he still believed in, but only just. Perhaps real justice wasn't on earth but in the next life, and that is where his hopes were now. He wondered what Emma was thinking now and whether she still believed his innocence. He hoped that she wasn't feeling guilty because she had stopped him from leaving and giving himself up the night before he was recaptured.

When the guard brought him his morning food, he heard the soldier clear his throat and then spit. The plate of beans was pushed through the gap at the bottom of the cell door. It didn't matter whether the spit had found its intended target or was just meant for him to believe it had, because he had no stomach for food, contaminated or otherwise.

Later that day his thoughts were once again disturbed by the bellowing voice of Sergeant Crowe. 'I've been told to pass on some good news to you, Stanton. It seems that you are going to be around for a bit longer. The officer allocated to conduct your defence, not that you have any, from what I've been told, won't be here until the middle of next week. He's one of those officers who sits at a desk back East and would shit his pants if he saw an Injun. I expect he's been ordered to come out here on account that no one else will touch your case.' Stanton didn't make any comment.

It was amazing how much Crowe reminded him of the late Sergeant Nolan: not just the same powerful build, bull neck and reddened features, but also the same aggressive nature.

During the week that followed Elliott was given a steady string of reports about the various activities going on in preparation for the trial. The Judge Advocate was to be General Compton, who was in charge of his first trial and he would once again use Captain Owen Slattery to handle the prosecution case. The usual procedure was for the Judge Advocate to present the prosecution, but General Compton preferred to delegate this to another officer.

It was just two days before the trial when Crowe informed Elliott that his defence counsel had arrived at the fort, but didn't know his name. According to Crowe he didn't look too bright, but then again he couldn't recall many officers who did. Elliott tried to get a message to Hawky to tell him that he didn't blame him for falling for Everson's trickery, but he was told that Hawky had been loaned to Fort Johnson and wasn't expected back until after the trial.

It was late afternoon when Elliott woke from a short sleep and was startled when he realized that someone was watching him from behind the cell bars. He didn't recognize the man at first. He was much thinner than the last time they had met, almost gaunt, and appeared to have aged dramatically. One thing that hadn't changed was that same look of hate. Colonel Danvers continued to stare at him for several more minutes with unblinking eyes. Elliott wouldn't have been surprised if his watcher was wishing every kind of hell on him. There was nothing that Elliott could say that would ease the pain of a man who had lost a daughter and a wife in such a short time. The colonel gave a twisted smile and left without speaking a single word.

Shortly after the colonel's departure Sergeant Crowe came to his cell with Lieutenant Robert Teal, the officer who had been assigned to defend him.

Neither Elliott nor the other young Lieutenant said anything until Crowe had walked away from the cell, then the two men gripped each other like long-lost brothers. Robert Teal had been his best buddy at West Point and his arrival lifted Elliott from the despair that he had felt since being brought back to the fort. The Teals were one of the wealthiest families in America, but Robert Teal was just about as ordinary as a man could be. He looked boyish compared to Elliott despite being born in the same year. Teal had specialized in army law since leaving West Point and had been fascinated by legal matters since he was a boy, but had an adventurous streak that made him a natural for military service. He was due to join an active post in a few months time, but when he heard the name of his old friend being mentioned he pulled a few strings to get assigned to the case.

The two men discussed old times, and it must have sounded odd for Crowe when he heard the frequent bursts of laughter coming from the cell before the two friends finally got down to the serious business of the trial.

'You should be aware, Elliott, that I have never taken part in a trial such as yours, but then again you don't have any choice, my old friend. I have spoken to Colonel Sedden who has replaced Colonel Danvers and he told me that the trial goes ahead in two days time come what may.'

'Have you thought what defending me might do to your career, Robert?' asked Elliott, concerned that his own bad fortune might in some way harm Robert Teal.

'The point is I was asked to defend you, Elliott,' Teal lied. 'So the way I see it, I am helping the army out of a sticky situation, so why should it harm me? I know you are innocent of the first charge but I have got to ask you if you killed the Sergeant.'

'No I didn't and that's the simple truth. Sergeant Nolan invited me to escape and provided me with a horse and offered me a head start before they came after me with the intention of killing me.'

'I'm sorry for having to ask you that, Elliott, but you might have killed him in self-defence.'

Elliott had told Teal about his encounter with Nolan's brother and that someone at the fort had hired him. It had been preying on his mind that he hadn't mentioned killing Bollinger. 'But there is something else that you should know,' said Elliott.

'Unless it is going to help your cause

in some way then I suggest that you keep it to yourself,' Teal advised.

Elliott remained silent and Teal took out some papers from a document case and set up an ink pot, into which he dipped a quill and started writing.

Teal read though his notes and sighed before speaking. 'I agree with you that Sergeant Nolan's death may be related to Eleanor's rape, but it's going to be difficult proving the connection. I have studied the papers from the first trial and the thing that was so damning for you was this business about your missing button. Have you still no idea how that could have happened. I must say that Everson didn't put up a very good show on your behalf. I have been wondering if perhaps Eleanor could have been trying to shake you from your unconsciousness and pulled off the button. What do you think?'

'It's possible, but I've been over it in mind and I'm convinced that the button wasn't missing when I was arrested.'

Teal asked Elliott to tell him every detail about the day of the rape, the arrest and Nolan's exact words when he was allowed to escape. Teal had already seen Everson but the man was less than helpful. As far as Everson was concerned, Stanton was guilty of all charges and he knew of no evidence that could help him.

Teal wanted Elliott's permission to call Emma as a witness so that she could testify that Elliott had planned to give himself up, but Elliott wasn't prepared to put her through the ordeal of testifying. He feared that the prosecution would claim that she was lying because she was his lover, and she might be branded for the rest of her life in a way that was worse than what the Indians had done to her.

It was late evening when Teal finally left Elliott's cell armed with his scribbled notes and made his way to his temporary quarters to prepare his flimsy case.

He was certain of one thing and that

was that Elliott was completely innocent, but unless he could work a
miracle, a good man and a real friend
would soon be dead.

17

The atmosphere in the court seemed less tense to Elliott than during his previous trial and he thought it might be due to the fact that the verdict was even more clear-cut this time. The only unfamiliar face to Elliott was that of Colonel Edwin P. Sedden, the new commanding officer who had taken over from Danvers. Teal had told him that Danvers would be leaving the fort after the trial, but Elliott guessed that his friend really meant after the execution.

The Judge Advocate's warning about clearing the court if there was any disturbance or interruptions looked to have worked as the court listened in silence as the charges were read out.

Teal's opening presentation was impressive as he sought the court's permission to review the original rape charge, claiming that the two cases were linked. The members of the panel were obviously taken by surprise and the court room was filled with muffled mutterings.

The Judge Advocate was also surprised and interrupted Teal. 'I take it that you are familiar with the previous court martial, Lieutenant.'

'I am, sir.'

'Then you must be aware of the fact that Miss Danvers was clutching a button which she had ripped from the accused's uniform during what must have been a violent struggle.'

'Yes sir, but it is my contention that this must have happened when Miss Danvers was trying to shake Lieutenant Stanton out of his unconsciousness that had resulted from a blow from behind by the real rapist.'

'Lieutenant, I hope that any defence that you are going to offer relating to the other charge is not based on speculation and fantasy. Now let us proceed to the murder charge case, unless you have some real evidence to present to us.'

Captain Slattery smiled as he looked across at Teal, but at least the young officer was trying his best and it might make the proceedings more interesting than last time.

Teal wasn't surprised at being admonished by the court. It might have been different had Everson made the same suggestion, but the court would be influenced by the fact that Elliott now stood accused of murder.

Teal told the court that Lieutenant Stanton had been allowed to escape and this was supported by the fact that the duty guard did not stop him from riding out of the fort.

Teal reminded the court that Sergeant Nolan was an extremely powerfully-built man who had been the victor in many bar room brawls, and it was inconceivable that he could have been overpowered by a much lighter man such as Lieutenant Stanton. Teal was temporarily encouraged as he watched members of the panel take notes, including the Judge Advocate. He hoped that Captain Slattery had taken the case lightly and not done any research into Elliott's background.

Slattery read through some papers as he prepared to question Elliott, a move clearly designed to put pressure on him. He finally delivered his opening question. 'Lieutenant Stanton, have you ever had reason to reprimand guards for sleeping on duty?'

'Yes, sir.'

'So on the day that you escaped the guards could have been bored and simply dozed off?'

'Yes, sir.'

'Lieutenant Teal has told us that the late Sergeant Nolan was a powerfully built man and fearsome brawler and I believe that to be true. Is it also true that you were a champion boxer at West Point and that you have defeated a number of men much more physically powerful than yourself.'

'Yes, sir.'

'Lieutenant, were you frightened of Sergeant Nolan?'

'No, sir.'

'So, if you had ever been involved in a fight with Sergeant Nolan you would have felt that your superior boxing skills and the fact that you were a younger and fitter man would have compensated for the physical differences and you might well have got the better of the Sergeant.'

'Yes, sir.'

Captain Owen J. Slattery had done his research and destroyed the slim defence that Teal had presented.

As Teal prepared himself to question Elliott he was distracted by a commotion caused by two men who had just entered the courtroom. He guessed correctly that one of them was Hawky; the other was a trooper and they had obviously been riding hard judging by their dusty clothes and sweaty faces.

Hawky gestured towards him and Teal asked for a recess while he talked to the men who he believed might have some fresh evidence.

General Compton begrudgingly allowed Teal thirty minutes, but it was long enough for him to hear what Hawky and Trooper Collins had to say. He decided that he would call them as witnesses, along with another man who he had noticed was already in court.

Hawky and Trooper Collins gave their testimony which was unchallenged by Slattery, except that he got Hawky to admit to being on very friendly terms with Elliott. The Judge Advocate gave a weary sigh before addressing Teal. 'So your new evidence, Lieutenant Teal, amounts to Trooper Collins hearing some vague statement from a drunken Sergeant Nolan about the button not being missing from Stanton's uniform at the time of his arrest. Added to that we have just heard from our Indian friend, Hawky, that Lieutenant Everson told him about the missing button the night before the accused was recaptured. Your next witness had better have something more useful to say.'

The mutterings around the court were heard again when Teal called Lieutenant Everson to the stand.

'Lieutenant Everson, is it true that you once had a strong personal relationship with Miss Eleanor Danvers?'

Everson was surprised by the question and looked towards the Judge Advocate and then Captain Slattery as though expecting one of them to intervene. They both remained silent and Teal repeated the question, to which Everson replied, 'I did see Miss Danvers occasionally when our families met on social occasions.'

'Is it true that you were hoping to become engaged to Miss Danvers before she came out here with her father and met Lieutenant Stanton?'

'No, it was never that serious,' replied Everson, clearly shaken by the tone of the questions from Teal.

'I think you are lying, Lieutenant, and I am certain that if I call Colonel Danvers, he will tell the court that you were having a serious relationship with his daughter. I'll ask you again. Were you hoping to become engaged to Miss Danvers?'

'Yes,' Everson admitted and fidgeted in his seat, clearly embarrassed by being forced to alter his reply.

'Thank you,' said Teal and continued, 'Did you ever tell Lieutenant Stanton about your relationship during the considerable amount of time that you spent with him as his defence counsel?'

'No,' replied Everson and lowered his head to avoid eye contact with Teal.

'How odd,' said Teal, who then paused and looked at the members of the board, hoping that the point had registered with those who would decide if Elliott would live or die. 'So you didn't think that it was unethical not to disclose this former relationship to the man you were representing at such an important trial?'

'No,' Everson answered as his discomfort continued.

'What did you mean when you told

Hawky that you had uncovered some new evidence about the missing button?'

'Nothing, it was just something that I made up to get him to lead us to where Stanton was. Everyone knew how incriminating the missing button was and I was willing to tell a lie if it meant bringing Stanton back to face justice.'

Teal shook his head and gave a faint smile before he continued. 'I will remind you that you are under oath, and ask you if you have any knowledge that supports the claims made here today that Lieutenant Stanton's tunic had no buttons missing when he was arrested and that it must have been cut off later. In other words, the button that Eleanor Danvers was clutching came from some other person's uniform and not Lieutenant Stanton's.'

Everson turned to the panel before replying. 'I have no such knowledge and I believe that the button came from Stanton's tunic.'

'Thank you, Lieutenant, no further questions.'

'Is that it, Lieutenant Teal?' asked the Judge Advocate who was beginning to appear bored with the proceedings.

'Yes, sir.'

The Judge Advocate looked up at the large clock on the wall to his right and then asked Captain Slattery if he had any comment on the new disclosures presented by Teal.

Captain Slattery had been reading some private papers unrelated to the case and the Judge Advocate's question had taken him by surprise, but he did not show any embarrassment as he replied, 'As you have already summarized very well, General, the evidence of the first two witnesses is hardly convincing and is not substantiated in any way. We have heard the testimony of Lieutenant Everson, a man who did his best to defend the accused at the first trial. Quite frankly I think the attempt to link the two crimes is pure fiction.'

'I am inclined to agree,' added the

Judge Advocate. 'The court will be adjourned for one hour and when we reconvene I would expect that the case will be concluded quite quickly.'

During the adjournment Teal had made another unsuccessful appeal to Elliott to allow him to call Emma as a witness, even though he doubted if the Judge Advocate would allow an adjournment while she was brought to the fort.

* * *

When the court reconvened Teal reminded them that Lieutenant Stanton had been an officer with an impeccable record and that he had sworn on oath that he planned to give himself up. The statement was greeted with a smirk from the prosecution counsel and laughter from some in the courtroom when a man called out cynically, 'Sure he was.'

Teal had at least expected the members of the board to retire and discuss the case, but following a brief huddled conversation amongst the panel members, the Judge Advocate banged his hammer on the desk and announced that he was ready to deliver his summing up and the verdict of the court. The courtroom was in total silence as the Judge Advocate started to speak.

'The defence has tried and failed to present this sad case as having a complicated linkage to the rape of Eleanor Danvers, of which the accused already stands guilty. But this case is a simple one of an evil man who deliberately murdered a comrade in order to escape rather than serve his punishment. He has shown no remorse for his evil doings and this court finds Elliott James Stanton guilty as charged and is hereby sentenced to face execution. The findings of this court are subject to ratification and the prisoner will be held in custody here at Fort Isaac until the legal process has been completed. Does the prisoner have anything to say to the court?'

'No sir,' Elliott replied, but he was not heard as those gathered roared out a loud cheer.

When Lieutenant Teal left the cells that evening after spending many hours with his friend he couldn't remember a time in his life when he had felt so sad. He had explained to Elliott that it might take many weeks before ratification would be complete. Teal would be returning to his office back East in a couple of days and planned to discuss the case with colleagues, but he had warned Elliott that it was highly unlikely that anything could be done. He had offered to go and see Emma, but Elliott had since decided against making any contact with Emma in order to explain everything to her. He believed that it would be better if she felt the worst of him because she might find it easier to cope with after she discovered that he was dead.

★   ★   ★

It was exactly five weeks since the end of the trial when Elliott was taken to Colonel Sedden's office to receive the news that the verdict had been ratified and that he would be executed by firing squad at the fort in three days time. Colonel Sedden seemed a fair man and explained that he didn't have any opinion about the case and asked if Elliott had any arrangements that he wished to make. Elliott told him that he had already arranged things, but he was pleased when the colonel told him that Robert Teal was expected at the fort the day before the execution.

The word of the ratification soon spread around the fort, but Elliott was no longer subjected to the abuse from the guards and in recent weeks some of them had commented that they thought he was innocent. It meant a lot to him to have that reassurance that not all men would be forever repulsed by the mention of his name.

★ ★ ★

When Robert Teal arrived back at Fort Isaac on the day before the execution he was surprised how well his friend looked. Colonel Sedden had allowed Teal permission to stay with Elliott for as long as he wanted and it was the early hours on the morning of the execution when he finally left the cell. Once he was outside the guardhouse Robert Teal sat on the steps and cried. He wasn't usually an emotional man but the thought that his friend — who had been a credit to the uniform he had worn — had been let down by the justice system and he would pay with his life, had finally got to him. The evening had been spent reliving yet more tales of West Point and Teal was pleased that he had helped Elliott's final hours pass with at least some happy memories. He had wanted to stay longer, but Elliott had insisted that he left him so that he could have some time to himself and the friends had said their final farewells. Elliott wanted tomorrow to be a private affair in which he would gather himself ready for the execution. There would be no blindfold for a man like Elliott when he faced the men who would fire the fatal shots.

18

Meg Jessell was one of a number of people who hadn't slept very well the night before the planned execution of Elliott Stanton. What she had been asked to do was simple enough but she was a born worrier and never felt comfortable in the presence of officers, particularly Colonel Danvers. He was a nice enough man and she felt really sorry for him since he'd lost his daughter and then that terrible thing with his wife. Meg hoped that what she had been asked to do might help him in some way, but she hadn't been told how it would. Her instructions had been quite clear, and she had spent the last hour or more since she had been awake looking at the clock. The first letter was to be delivered at eight o'clock and the other two after nine. Meg reminded herself of how important it was for the letters to be delivered in the right order and at the right time.

Meg was the sutler's daughter and had been a general sort of servant at the fort for nearly two years, but she was hoping that if Lieutenant Everson continued to show interest in her then she might not be cleaning for much longer.

Meg made her way towards Colonel Danvers' house feeling as nervous as a kitten. Delivering the first letter had been quite painless but it was the next one that she didn't like doing. It seemed an age before she heard some response to her knock and the Colonel opened the door. He was fully dressed in his best uniform and looked immaculate, but he appeared strained and hunched, no longer the commanding figure that he had been before tragedy struck.

'What is it, dear, have you come to clean?' he asked politely.

'No, sir, I've been asked to deliver this to you.'

He looked puzzled as he accepted the large white envelope from her.

'Oh, I see. Well thank you for your trouble.'

'Thank you, sir,' Meg replied before hurrying away and then mentally reprimanded herself for offering her thanks to the colonel, realizing that she had nothing to thank him for.

★ ★ ★

It was barely five minutes later when Meg was passing the Colonel's quarters again, having completed her errands, when she heard the single shot. She stopped and watched as a trooper ran into the house and then reappeared just as quickly, shouting out what he had discovered to the other soldiers who had come to investigate. The nightmare was over for one man.

★ ★ ★

Colonel Sedden was just beginning to read the letter that had been delivered to him by the pretty cleaning lady when his orderly, Lieutenant Craggs, rushed in and announced the death of Colonel Danvers. Sedden continued to read the letter which told him that Colonel Danvers had been sent an identical copy. The orderly stood in silence, surprised at the Colonel's apparent disregard for the dramatic news that he had just told him.

'Lieutenant Craggs, have you seen Captain Pearmain this morning?'

'Yes, sir, I saw him riding out of the fort about twenty minutes ago. He likes to exercise his horse several times a day.'

'Right, Lieutenant, I want you to take some men and arrest Lieutenant Everson. I'll meet you at the guard-house when I have finished dressing. You must tell the guards to stop the preparation for the execution and you are to order the release of Lieutenant Stanton. I'm afraid there has been a terrible mistake and Stanton is an innocent man. Oh, and Lieutenant, have someone get a tunic, hat, belt and pistol for Stanton and have them taken to the guardhouse.'

As Lieutenant Craggs raced away, puzzled by his orders but eager to carry them out, Colonel Sedden quickly read through Eloise Pearmain's letter again. She had left the fort yesterday supposedly to visit relatives back East, but not before she had arranged for the Jessel girl to deliver the three letters. The letter described how her husband, Captain Pearmain, had arrived home on the day of the rape with scratches on his hands and a button missing from his tunic. She also discovered blood on one of his uniforms on the day that Sergeant Nolan was murdered. Her husband had been besotted by his cousin Eleanor and she believed that he was both the rapist and the killer of Sergeant Nolan. She asked for Lieutenant Stanton's forgiveness at her not having the courage to reveal what she knew before now. Eloise Pearmain's final duty to her husband was to warn him about the other two letters and so give him a chance to escape. At the end of the letter she revealed that Lieutenant Everson had known Pearmain had removed the button from Stanton's tunic but had been too frightened to report it. She explained that her husband was blackmailing Everson over something he had done that would have brought disgrace on Everson's family had it been revealed.

*　*　*

Elliott looked at the prison clock for the fifth time in as many minutes and saw that it was just thirty-two minutes before he would be led out. He had already declined a visit by the chaplain. Elliott wasn't a disbeliever but didn't want to hear the minister praying for his forgiveness. He had nothing to ask God for other than to look after his ma and help her through the extra shame that would come her way. When he heard the disturbance and saw Lieutenant Craggs, he figured they were coming to take him out earlier than planned.

'Guard,' Craggs shouted. 'Colonel Sedden has ordered that the preparation for the execution be stopped. He'll be here shortly to take charge of things. In the meantime prepare the other cell for Lieutenant Everson, who is being held under arrest outside. Now, open the cells and release Lieutenant Stanton. He's an innocent man and there's been a terrible mistake.'

Stanton was reminded of the moment when Nolan had invited him to go free. He knew that whatever was happening here wasn't the same and that this was for real. He didn't know where Everson fitted into all of this, but it didn't surprise him.

Elliott looked on in disbelief as the guard fumbled with the keys and Colonel Sedden, who had just arrived, stepped forward and offered him the letter. 'I think you ought to read this, Lieutenant. I'm truly sorry for what you have been through.'

Elliott found it hard to take it in that the man who he would have probably regarded as the most unlikely suspect had been responsible for such evil.

'Sir, does Colonel Danvers know what his nephew has done?' Elliott asked. 'He'll be devastated.'

'I'm afraid the poor man is past caring,' Sedden replied. 'He blew his brains out when he discovered the truth about what happened to his daughter. It must have been just too much for him after losing his wife as well.'

Elliott shook his head and sighed, knowing that Colonel Danvers had been a victim as well as himself.

Colonel Sedden picked up the gun belt and pistol from the desk and handed them to Elliott. 'If you feel up to it, Lieutenant, then I would like you lead the party to go after Pearmain. The sentry said he left the fort about thirty minutes ago and was heading on the trail to the mountains or the river. My guess is that he will try and cross the river. I have sent someone to get Hawky so that he can join you on the hunt.'

'I'm fit enough, sir, and I promise you that I will not be returning until we have caught Pearmain.'

'Good man,' said the Colonel and placed a hand on Elliott's shoulder.

Elliott put on the jacket that had been handed to him and then strapped on the belt and weapon before following the Colonel outside where he saw the party of ten men who were already mounted. Elliott glared at Everson, but Everson avoided eye contact as he was led into the guardhouse.

Elliott had just placed his foot in the stirrup ready to mount the horse when a breathless trooper came running from the direction of Hawky's bunkhouse.

'Colonel, Hawky's dead. He's had his throat cut,' the trooper gasped.

'Good God, Pearmain is an absolute monster,' said a shocked Colonel Sedden who was quite certain who was

Hawky's killer. 'Make sure that you catch him, Lieutenant, but be careful — and good luck.'

Robert Teal had arrived at the prison to await the execution and could only shout with excitement as he watched a fully-armed Elliott preparing to ride out.

'Elliott, what has happened?'

'Your friend's a free man, Lieutenant,' said Sedden. 'That's what has happened. I'll explain it all to you in a moment.'

Teal shook his head in disbelief and smiled as the party galloped away.

Elliott felt a surge of energy as he pushed his mount to take up the lead position. He had been so close to being executed and now against all the odds his name had been cleared. The thought of Hawky's death added to his anger that Pearmain, a fellow officer, had caused so much destruction. Pearmain had been full of charm and had helped Elliott settle in when he had first arrived at the fort and had given no clues that he was capable of such evil. Pearmain would have been desperate to flee from the fort once he had read the letter from his wife, but had taken the time to murder the man who would have picked up his trail.

Elliott knew most of the men who galloped behind him. They must have been as surprised as he was at the way things had developed. Some of them had likely been amongst those who had jeered him a short time ago and now they were under his command.

* * *

It was just over twenty minutes after the party had left the fort when the memory of the last time he had ridden this trail returned to Elliott, and he suddenly raised his arm to signal those behind him to stop.

'Corporal Turner, there's a small section of woodland to the west of this trail about a mile away. I'm going to take a detour and approach the woods from the other side. I want you and the rest of the men to keep on this trail to the river. If you hear any gunfire then bring the men back to the woods; otherwise keep heading for the river.'

Corporal Turner thought the Lieutenant was making a bad move, but orders were orders and he led the men away at a gallop.

It was a gamble being played on a hunch, and if he was wrong he might miss the chance to be there when the troopers caught up with Pearmain. It was going to be much more difficult to capture him if he managed to reach the river. He was the sort of man who would survive on the run by using his charm and he would have some influential friends who might even help him later.

Elliott dismounted at the entrance to the woods and drew his pistol as he edged forward. Each step he took on the dry leaves and pine needles resulted in the sound of a loud crunch. Perhaps it was a mistake to come in here alone.

A safer plan would have been to split the party in two and approach the woods from both sides, but it was too late for that now. Going it alone was dangerous but it gave him the chance to settle this personally. Although Pearmain was a powerfully built man, Elliott was confident that he would get the better of him in an open fight. The way he felt at the moment he would have tackled three men if it meant getting Pearmain. He froze as he heard the sound of movement ahead of him, and the familiar jangle that came from a horse shaking its head. He considered calling out to invite the other occupant of the woods to declare himself. One thing was certain, if it was Pearmain there would be only one thing he would want to do and that was to kill Elliott. In the split second that Elliott spotted Pearmain's distinctive custom-built saddle, he felt the blow to his head and pitched forward onto the ground. He was dazed and unable to recover before Pearmain had dived on top of him, brandishing the same long-bladed knife that had been used to stab the unsuspecting Hawky. Elliott felt the breath of Pearmain on his neck as the killer prepared to slice the knife into his throat. He braced himself and then used the back of his head to butt Pearmain full in the face causing Pearmain to fall back. Despite the force of the blow, Pearmain staggered to his feet and wiped his hand across his bloodied face before he threw the knife at Elliott, but it missed its target and fell some yards away. He hadn't wanted to shoot Stanton, fearing that the sound of gunfire might attract the attention of his other pursuers, but now he drew his pistol.

Pearmain prepared to kill his second man that day as he glowered at Stanton. 'Your luck has just about run out, Stanton. You were a fool wasting a chance to escape after I told Nolan to let you go. I was hoping that Nolan's brother would have finished you off for me, but he must have taken my money and run. I never understood what Eleanor saw in you, but some women have strange tastes. Now turn over. I don't want to shoot you in the back, it's not very honourable.' Pearmain laughed at his own hypocrisy.

Stanton's right hand had been trapped under his body when he fell, and as he pressed his hand into the earth to roll over he felt the gun. He was in exactly the same spot where Bollinger's pistol had been buried amongst the dead leaves. Elliott rolled and fired in one swift motion. He would never forget the look of surprise on Pearmain's face before he fell to the ground. Elliott got to his feet and fired three times in quick succession to signal to his men. Pearmain lay groaning, but he would be dead before the main party reached the woods.

Elliott dropped to his knees as it sunk in that the nightmare was over, but there was no feeling of elation, only sadness, as he remembered those dead back at the fort: the colonel, who at least was at peace and Hawky, the man without whose help he would not soon be thinking of starting a new life.

When Elliott and the party returned to the fort with Pearmain's body he had wanted to go and see Emma, but he had to stay and help with the inquiry into what had happened. General Alpheus W. Thomas had been doing an inspection of the forts and had taken charge of the inquiry. Elliott told him everything that had happened, including how Bollinger and Travan had died and the events in Jerome in which he helped Makin escape. Elliott was cleared of any wrongdoing and warmly praised by the general for the way he had conducted himself throughout the whole sorry business.

* * *

So it was three days after the day he was to have been executed when he was ready to ride out to the Ashley place, but not before he attended a special parade in his honour.

Colonel Sedden stood between Elliott and Lieutenant Teal as he prepared to address an almost full turnout of the garrison, and only those on guard duty were missing from the parade. Elliott was immaculately dressed in ceremonial uniform and his hair had been cut to its normal length.

He stood tall and proud, just the way he had done on the day that he had passed out of West Point watched by his parents.

When Colonel Sedden started his tribute there was total silence amongst those gathered.

'Lieutenant Stanton was subjected to a gross injustice but displayed a level of courage and fortitude as much as any soldier could have done in battle. He is a credit to the US Cavalry and I will be recommending him for a special citation. He also had the friendship of Hawky who was a great servant to the US army. Hawky was a credit not only to his own nation, but also this great nation of ours. There is also another very brave person who is not here today but deserves a special mention. If it wasn't for the courage shown by Eloise Pearmain, who had the misfortune to be married to an evil man, then Lieutenant Stanton would be dead and her monstrous husband would still be alive.'

Stanton's thoughts echoed the Colonel's and he would be eternally grateful to Eloise Pearmain for her courage and honesty.

Elliott had attended the funeral of Hawky who was buried with full military honours and Teal said that he would arrange for Hawky's widow to receive compensation and a pension from the army. Teal also told him that Sergeant Crowe was to be dismissed from the service for his brutal behaviour towards Stanton and that Everson was to face a court martial and would probably be sent to prison and dismissed from the service.

When Elliott rode out of the fort he

received a barrage of cheers from the men who had come to realize what he had endured. He had told the Colonel that he needed time to think over his future. He planned to take extended leave, and would visit his ma and recover the medal that he had left buried near his pa. But first he had to call on a very special lady by the name of Emma.

THE END